A Girl Called
Blue

Marita Conlon-McKenna

THE O'BRIEN PRESS
DUBLIN

First published 2003 by The O'Brien Press Ltd,
20 Victoria Road, Dublin 6, Ireland.
Tel: +353 1 4923333; Fax: +353 1 4922777
E-mail: books@obrien.ie
Website: www.obrien.ie

ISBN: 0-86278-850-1

British Library Cataloguing-in-Publication Data
Conlon-McKenna, Marita
A girl called Blue
1.Orphans - Juvenile fiction
2.Orphanages - Juvenile fiction
3.Children's stories
I.Title
823.9'14[J]

1 2 3 4 5 6 7 8 9 10
03 04 05 06 07 08 09 10

Editing, typesetting, layout, design: The O'Brien Press Ltd
Printing: CPD Books

Dedication

For all those who had no mother or father to
care for them.

A sincere thank you to Michael O'Brien and all at
The O'Brien Press, especially to my dedicated editor,
Íde ní Laoghaire; to Emma Byrne for creating a wonderful cover,
and to Caitríona Magner for her help and enthusiasm. Thanks
also to Carol Sheridan of the Public Relations department of
Iarnród Éireann for her assistance.

As always, my deepest thanks go to my ever-loyal and supportive
family: my husband James and my children, Amanda,
Laura, Fiona and James. And a special mention for my dog, Mitzi,
who sat patiently by my feet through the writing of this book.

CONTENTS

CHAPTER 1

Larch Hill

Kick! Kick! Kick! Blue kicked the toe of her boot against the leg of the heavy mahogany table. She was fed up waiting in the cold, dreary parlour for the Hickeys to come. It was sunny outside, warm even, not that the heavy brocade curtains and lace nets that framed the bay window allowed any of the spring sunshine to spill into the damp, musty room. Blue hated this parlour, with its smell of waxy furniture polish, hated having to sit still in the chair waiting to be picked up and taken out of Larch Hill children's home for the day.

She had washed her hair and brushed it till it shone, scrubbed her hands and nails and put on her clean, pleated skirt, good white blouse and navy cardigan. She was ready. Now she just needed Mr and Mrs Hickey to come and collect her.

She really liked the Hickeys. Mrs Hickey was very pretty with long blond hair and peach-coloured lipstick. She laughed a lot and smelled of sweet perfume. She had let Blue try on her high-heeled shoes and sprayed her with the same sweet scent when Blue visited their redbrick home on the other side of the city. Mrs Hickey talked about her sisters and their families and how much she wanted a family of her own. They had taken her to the Metropole cinema to see *Mary Poppins* a few weeks ago and Blue sat in the darkness between them, entranced, laughing when they laughed and clapping like they did at the end of the matinee show. It was like being sandwiched between two parents. Blue was ecstatic. Afterwards they took her to tea in a restaurant nearby and she cleared her plate of the sandwiches and scones they ordered, and politely sipped her cup of tea.

Mr Hickey had said it was great to see a girl with such a good appetite. When he was driving her back to the children's home he had pushed a shiny half crown coin into Blue's hand, telling her to treat herself to something nice.

She wondered what they had planned for today. Maybe they'd go to the cinema again, or, since it was sunny, perhaps a walk in the park, the one with the lake and quacking ducks that her friends Lil and Jess had told her about. She waited, peering out through the curtains every few minutes for any sign of them. They should be here by now. The time was ticking away, wasted. At this rate she'd have no time to go anywhere, do anything. It just wasn't fair.

The parlour door opened and she automatically jumped up. But it wasn't them. It was only Sister Monica, 'Monkey' as the others called her. But Blue liked her. Sometimes she thought Sister Monica was her only friend in the whole world. She was an old nun, retired from the African missions, and she was in charge of opening the door to visitors.

'There you are, child.'

Blue nodded.

'They're not coming,' said the nun gently. 'I'm sorry, but Sister Regina got word a while ago that they won't be coming to take you out today.'

Blue swallowed hard, pretending it didn't matter, that it didn't hurt.

'Mr Hickey's busy. They don't have time for a visit.'

Not coming today … 'Are they coming next Sunday?'

She could see the look of pity in the elderly nun's eyes as Sister Monica searched for an excuse. She always told the truth. Now she said nothing.

'The Sunday after?'

'Mrs Hickey's not that well, Bernadette. Perhaps it's better for everyone that this is the end of it. There's no point in going on with something that's not going to work out, or that people have had second thoughts about. Perhaps it's better this way.'

'They're not coming to see me ever again.' She blinked furiously. She didn't want the nun to see her cry.

'I'm sorry, child, but I don't think so,' Sister Monica replied.

Blue gave the table an almighty kick, the sound filling the silent room and hanging between them. She waited for the nun to admonish her.

'You'd better go upstairs and take off your coat,' Sister Monica suggested. 'Change out of your good clothes. Then you might go up and help in the nursery. I know they could do with an extra pair of hands.'

Blue got to her feet and with a cold, empty feeling in the pit of her stomach she ran out the door.

* * *

It was noisy and stuffy in the huge upstairs room where the babies slept and spent the endless hours of their day. Though the tall window was open, the smell of sour milk and nappies in need of changing assailed her. Big Ellen held a bawling child in her arms and was walking him up and down, trying to soothe him.

'I think he must be teething or something,' she said, bouncing him in her arms. 'The poor little pet!'

Three or four toddlers were standing up in their cots, pulling at the bars, rocking themselves, ready to join in the fracas and demand attention too.

'It's mighty hot up here,' complained Blue, fanning her face.

'I thought you were going out today?'

'I was supposed to,' Blue explained, 'but they didn't show.'

She didn't mind telling Big Ellen the truth, as she was one of the nicest people in the whole place. The older girl loved working with the babies and toddlers, forever washing and feeding and changing them, and had confided to Blue that when she was old enough she was going to try and become a nurse. Blue didn't know how she put up with all the work.

'I think Billy needs changing,' suggested Big Ellen.

Blue gritted her teeth as she lifted the bald, whingeing six-month-old from his cot. He was like a little old man, she thought, and she wrinkled her nose as she carried the whimpering baby over to the changing table. He stared at her, big-eyed, kicking his chubby legs against her, wanting her to play with him. But she wasn't in the mood, not today.

'Ah, Blue, will you give him a little tickle or a wee kiss or something!' Big Ellen watched from a distance as Blue cleaned him, replacing the soaked and dirty towelling-cloth nappy with a fresh, dry one and dumping the soiled one in the bucket.

What a way to spend her Sunday. She should be sitting on a bench in the park or playing on the swings, or feeding the ducks, not stuck here minding these babies.

When she lifted him back up Billy grabbed at her hair, and, despite herself, Blue held him close and jigged him up and down, making him laugh and gurgle.

It wasn't his fault nobody wanted him. She kissed his soft, baby skin. He smelt lovely now. She looked around the room. She, too, had spent the first two years of her life in this very spot, crying to be picked up and howling when she was put down. Chasing the thought away, she hugged Billy close.

'You poor little sausage,' she consoled, spinning him round the room in her arms. 'You poor little sausage.'

By tea-time Blue was exhausted. She'd helped Big Ellen bathe and feed the fourteen babies in the room and her blouse was stained and wet. She'd hoped to get down and have her tea before all those who had been out got back, but she now realised she would be lucky to be in time to get anything to eat at all.

At last, she slid on to the bench in the dining room between Jess and Mary. Jess, back from her day out, was showing off the half-crown coin she'd got from Eileen, the woman who came to visit her twice a year. Blue pulled the two remaining slices of bread on to her plate. The sliced pan was curling at the edges already as she spread it with a layer of greasy margarine. But she was starving, and she gobbled it down as fast as she could.

CHAPTER 2

Molly

Blue tossed and turned in her bed that night, unable to sleep. She was still upset about the Hickeys, wondering why they hadn't visited her. Maybe she wasn't pretty enough, or clever enough. Maybe she wasn't chatty enough, like her friends Jess and Mary and Lil. She sighed. She was just too ordinary.

The room was warm and stuffy and filled with the coughs and snores of the fifteen girls she shared the dormitory with. She could hear Mary grinding her teeth, and Annie rambling and talking in her sleep as usual. She sighed. The girl should be used to the orphanage by now.

She herself had been in Saint Brigid's home, Larch Hill, since she was a baby. She had no memory of any other place. This was her home, the nuns who ran it her guardians. She had spent twelve years, five months and fifteen days here.

The children's home had been open for over a hundred years, housing orphans and children whose parents could no longer look after them. The nuns always called it St Brigid's after its patron saint, but the children who lived there referred to it as Larch Hill. Other people called it 'the orphanage' which was wrong, as lots of the kids in Larch Hill did have parents, a mother or a father, even if they rarely saw them.

In the quiet of night, Blue wondered about all the other children down through the years who had slept in this room, and, like her, spent their whole life in Larch Hill. She could sense their ghosts in the corridor, their shadows at the window. She was not afraid of them.

Sometimes she wondered about her mother. Was she still alive or was she dead? Did she think of her? Remember her? Blue had been given into the care of the nuns when she was only a few days old and had no idea of her history or who she really was. It was the nuns who had named and baptised her Bernadette Lourdes Una O'Malley. The nuns had fed her and taught her to walk and talk and survive the hardships of life in a crowded children's home. She never had any relations come to check on her or see how she was doing, and gradually she gave up any hope of them. Because her mother had not signed the papers, she could not be adopted. Perhaps one day her mother would come back and reclaim her and call her her own. Till then she was just another of the 'orphan kids', as the other girls in the school they attended down the street called them.

She kicked the blanket off, stretching her legs and toes and yawning. She just couldn't get to sleep. She tried to push thoughts of Mr and Mrs Hickey from her mind. There was no point in being upset about them, as that wouldn't change a thing. She bent down and scrabbled under the mattress. She pulled out her precious yellow magazine and, punching her pillow, curled up and began to read. The street light outside was bright enough – Blue felt lucky it was placed just outside her dormitory as it gave her the chance to look at her favourite magazine undisturbed at night. Sister Monica had given her this magazine when she was eight years old. 'I think you might like this, child,' she'd said.

Like! Why, she had never seen anything like it. The magazine was called *National Geographic* and it had a picture of Africa, where Sister Monica had worked on the missions, on the yellow front cover.

The inside was filled with pictures of places all around the world and the people who lived there. Blue had studied it from cover to cover, over and over again, reading every precious word.

She knew every picture, every photograph, the colours, the faces, the animals, the landscapes – the rich detail filled her lonely heart. The magazine was like magic, somehow it could take her away from where she was. For a time she could live her life in another place, become another person, far from this grey, sad place.

She curled up, the magazine half-hidden under her blanket as she began to read and to gaze at the photographs. Teza's African face smiled back at Blue as she carried water from the river to her family.

But there was a sudden interruption. 'Blue! Blue, what are you doing?'

It was Molly, the new little girl who slept in the bed beside hers. She was only six years old and had been placed in Larch Hill by her father, who had gone to England to look for work following the death of her mother four months ago. She looked like she'd woken from a bad dream.

'Are you all right, Molly?'

The little girl shook her head, wordless, the tears beginning.

Blue sighed. 'Do you want to come in with me for a few minutes?'

The dark head nodded and Blue put down her magazine and pulled back the blanket as Molly jumped in beside her.

'Do you want to look at the pictures?'

Molly nodded, yawning.

Blue turned the pages slowly, explaining in a whisper one or two of the photographs, but it was late and she could see that Molly was too tired to take it in.

'Would you like me to tell you a story instead?'

'My mammy told me stories,' the little girl said solemnly. 'Every night.'

'Well, then, that's what I'll do. I'll tell you a story and when I'm finished you'll get back into your own bed and go to sleep, promise!'

Molly agreed.

'Once upon a time in a house in the big woods there lived three bears …' she began as Molly snuggled against her, the small body gradually relaxing. In time, Molly would get used to it, to being on her own and having no mammy or daddy to take care of her.

'… a big bear, a middle-sized bear and a little baby bear …'

CHAPTER 3

Rules and Regulations

The routine was the same, day in day out, for all the children living behind the high grey walls of Larch Hill: prayers, washing, early morning mass, a porridge breakfast, school; after school there were the classrooms to be cleaned, rosary beads to make, laundry work; older children had to help with the babies and little ones; finally there was some playtime in the yard, then homework and bed. These activities were punctuated by scanty meals. Sometimes it seemed to Blue that they were all being punished for something they didn't understand, something those in charge of them believed they had done – a big sin they or their parents had committed that no amount of prayer or hard work could ever wipe away.

The boredom and hard work made some kids cry all the time; others stopped talking, shutting themselves away in a secret world of their own. Some went crazy and kicked and screamed and fought until Sister Regina and the rest of the nuns got so cross with them they were removed from Larch Hill. There were frightening rumours of where these children were sent and the treatment they received.

'The looney bin! That's where Deirdre Byrne got sent,' Lil swore.

Blue had no intention of ending up in a place like that, and when she looked out at the big yard with its empty swings and slide and saw the little kids like Molly working instead of playing, she hardened her heart and buried her anger and used her yellow magazine to help her escape.

Monday and Friday were laundry days, Tuesday was mending and ironing, but Saturday was the worst – it was 'scrub day'. They had to clean the whole building from top to bottom, brushing, dusting, washing; tables had to be wiped and floors scrubbed, polished and waxed. Everyone had a job to do to keep the children's home spick and span.

Blue and Jess stood in Jerusalem corridor one Saturday. Three other girls had already brushed and washed the long, long stretch of wooden flooring and it was their job now to wax and polish it. It would take them forever.

'Come on, Jess, pass me the tin of polish,' instructed Blue.

Jess kicked it over towards her friend, then suddenly threw herself towards the floor after it. 'Hey, Blue, watch!' she called.

Up! Down! Over! Flip! Blue watched as Jess did cartwheel after cartwheel along the empty corridor, her body light as a feather.

'Go on, Blue! Try it!' urged Jess, back on her feet again.

Blue put down her polishing cloth, then placed her hands flat on the ground and tried to get the rest of her body to rise through the air.

'Ow!' She fell, almost hitting the wall.

'You're going too slow!' advised Jess, doing another three

cartwheels to show her. 'You have to do it fast, not think about it.'

It made Blue feel dizzy and clumsy watching Jess, with her long, skinny body and perfect balance, almost fly through the air.

'I just can't do it,' laughed Blue, as she collapsed again, crashing into a chair.

'It's so easy and you'll feel great!' enthused Jess. 'Here, I'll help you. Put your hands down and I'll hold your waist. Now, lift your legs and ...'

Blue began again, but collapsed in a fit of giggling. Too late she saw the long, black skirt of a nun's habit and heard the click of heavy black beads. It was Sister Regina, 'The Crow', the head nun. They were in trouble now.

'What are you two girls doing?' asked Sister Regina.

'Nothing, Sister,' they said in unison, standing up and trying to make themselves look presentable.

'I wouldn't call it nothing to have two big girls like yourselves tumbling around the corridor, showing off their knickers and falling on to convent property.'

Blue looked at the floor, feeling the giggles coming from right down inside her, not wanting to look at Jess in case she felt the same. She could feel herself starting to shake with silent laughter. Jess suddenly exploded.

'So, you girls think this is funny!' said Sister Regina solemnly. They could feel the shift in tone, and instantly all thoughts of giggling and messing were gone. 'Into my office!' she ordered.

Blue's heart sank. They were going to be punished.

Silently they marched down the empty corridor, across the hallway and down the next corridor that led to the head nun's study, watching as she took out her keys and unlocked the door.

'Inside,' she ordered.

The two of them stood, nervous and scared, in the middle of the room as the nun drew out her black leather strap.

'What are the rules here in Saint Brigid's?'

Blue sighed. There were so many rules and regulations in Larch Hill that it would take hours to list them all off. Rules about getting up, rules about using the bathroom, rules about being in time for mass, rules about school, rules about cleaning the school basins and classroom and yard, rules about doing the laundry, rules about minding the babies, about clearing the table, rules about going to bed, rules about not talking. There was a rule to cover every single thing you ever did.

'The rules are not to run or play in the corridors, Sister,' said Jess.

'And …'

'And we broke them,' added Blue.

The nun stared at them, considering. 'Hold out your hands,' she said finally.

Blue tried not to flinch as the strap rained down on her – one, two, three heavy blows. She blinked away the tears and cradled her hands under her arms as Sister Regina turned to Jess. A minute later it was over.

'Dismissed – and back to work,' said the nun, ignoring them now as they made for the door. Blue was barely able to turn the handle with the pain and stinging soreness in her hands.

They walked in silence along the ground floor and up the stairs to the bathroom, then raced to the sink and let the cold water run over their fingers and palms.

'Ow! Ow!' they moaned in unison.

'I hate her,' said Jess. 'We were only having fun. We weren't doing any harm.'

Blue leaned against the cool bathroom tiles. There was hardly a kid in the place who hadn't had a smack or a blow, or a lash of the black leather strap or the cane. It was something they were all used to, being black and blue, and sore.

'She's mad!' declared Jess. 'She hates us all, hates us being happy. She can't stand it!'

Everyone knew the nuns were strict, but Sister Regina was a total disciplinarian. Everybody was afraid of her, even some of the nuns.

'If I had a ma or a da or a big brother,' continued Jess, 'I'd tell them what she does to us. It's because we've nobody that she picks on us. She's a big bully. Blue, some day I'm going to just pack up and get out of here! You just wait and see. I'm saving Eileen's money and when I get my chance I'll take off and I won't come back.'

Blue said nothing. She didn't know how she'd bear it in Larch Hill if she hadn't Jess as her best friend.

CHAPTER 4

Wet-a-bed

Blue didn't know how it happened but bit by bit she found herself watching out for little Molly. At first she tried to pretend it was just because she pitied her, but after a while she realised it was more than that: she cared about her and wanted to protect her as if she was her own little sister. It was a bit like Mary, whose little brother Tommy was also in Larch Hill.

'She's always following you around,' joked Mary. 'She's like your shadow. Just like Tommy.'

Blue had smiled, secretly pleased, knowing that it was true. The two looked nothing like each other: Molly's dark curly hair and deep brown eyes were in total contrast to her own straight hair, wide face and blue eyes, yet there was something about the little girl that made Blue want to help her. It *was* almost like having a little sister.

She warned Lil and Mary and Jess to be kind to her and tried to get Molly to mix with the other girls her own age.

'Go on and play with them,' she begged one day. But Molly was shy and awkward, and hung back. 'Why won't you play hopscotch with the others, Molly? Go and have some fun with your friends,' she urged, wishing the little girl would take the first few steps to making new friends instead of always standing back, alone, in the schoolyard or the recreation room. But Molly just stood there, shy and quiet, her brown eyes looking sad and hurt as she watched all the others having fun.

'She's a strange little thing,' said Lil, 'but she'll settle.'

Blue wasn't so sure.

'Why can't I just play with you?' Molly asked Blue.

'Because you need to get to know the kids in your class, the ones your own age.'

'But I don't like them, and they don't like me.'

'You just don't know each other yet, that's all,' Blue sighed impatiently.

'Why does everyone call you Blue?' asked Molly, changing the subject.

'My real name is Bernadette Lourdes Una O'Malley,' Blue explained, 'but, because there were so many other girls called Bernadette and Bernie here, someone nicknamed me Blue when I was small. They said it was because I had the biggest and boldest blue eyes they ever saw! And the name stuck. But the nuns don't like it, of course.'

'I like it,' said Molly.

'Me too! Now, come on and we'll go and see if anyone is on the swing in the back yard.'

* * *

Early one morning, before the mass bell had sounded, Blue stretched under the blankets. Molly was still fast asleep, her dark curly hair spread out on the pillow, her eyes closed.

'Molly!' she whispered. 'Molly, wake up.'

Molly stirred, but curled up again immediately.

'Molly, you have to wake up!' she whispered more urgently.

Molly's eyes opened slowly, her face changing, her eyes scrunching up.

Blue wrinkled her nose. It was too late. Molly had wet the bed. She was in trouble again.

'Good morning!' Sister Carmel burst into the dormitory, yanking the curtains open. Tall and thin, she was much younger than the rest of the nuns. 'Out of bed immediately,' she ordered, 'or you'll all be late for mass.'

The room filled with groans and complaints as the cold morning air greeted the girls.

Throwing back her coverlet, Blue slowly got out of bed.

'Molly! Up at once!' ordered the nun, striding over. Cautiously the little girl sat up, her cheeks red, her hair tousled. The nun grabbed hold of the floral bed cover and the blanket and pulled them back.

'Ugh! Smelly!' shouted Joan Doherty, a big, pimply-faced girl who loved to jeer at anyone younger and weaker than her.

Sister Carmel tore all the clothes off the bed, revealing the yellow-stained sheets.

'I'm sorry, Sister,' whispered Molly, standing, shaking in her wet nightdress.

'Wet-a-bed! Wet-a-bed!' The call went up from Joan and her friends. 'Wet-a-bed! Wet-a-bed!'

'Leave her alone!' said Blue, wanting to go over and punch Joan in the jaw. 'She's only small. It was an accident.'

'She has accidents every night!' jeered Joan. 'She should sleep in a nappy with the babies upstairs.'

Blue could feel the anger flare in her stomach. Molly had enough problems without Joan making things worse.

'Come on, Molly,' she offered. 'I'll take you to the bathroom.'

'One minute, Bernadette,' interrupted the nun. 'Molly, strip the sheets off your bed and carry them down to the laundry room.'

Molly looked scared, like she was going to break down and cry. She pulled the sodden sheets off her bed and bundled them up in her arms. The room filled with the smell of urine as she walked out towards the landing.

'Disgusting!' sneered Joan.

Blue hated it, the daily humiliation of those who had wet their beds. She pitied Molly having to brave the jeers of the girls and the anger of the nuns. None of it was helping; constantly calling attention to Molly's problem only seemed to be making it worse. She could hear the cat-calls from other dormitories at the other transgressors as they formed a line, all armed with their smelly, wet bedclothes. Molly joined them. Blue was washed and dressed and brushing her hair by the time the little girl got back. She watched as Molly began to pull on her school skirt and blouse.

'Molly!' she warned, 'what about –'

'I've no time to wash, I'm already late for mass,' Molly interrupted. 'I'll just get into more trouble.'

'No!' insisted Blue. 'Come on, I'll take you to the bathroom and help you. Quick. Hurry up!'

Blue knew that the other kids in school and those who sat near Molly in the chapel were beginning to object to the strong smell coming from her.

The line of children for the washbasins had cleared by now, and Blue grabbed hold of a towel and some soap and soaped the little girl all over. Then she dried her briskly with the rough towel, before making her put on her underwear and uniform.

'Now, that's perfect,' she smiled, as she tidied Molly's hair with the brush.

Kneeling in the bench during morning mass she could guess what Molly was praying for. She could see it in her expression. Blue vowed to somehow try and help her to remember to wake up, get out of bed and go to the toilet.

CHAPTER 5

The Mystery Tour

They all screamed out the tune of the Beatles' new song 'She loves you', as Jimmy Mooney, the taxi driver, turned off the corner of Larch Hill and on to the Dublin Road, joining the cavalcade of taxis of every size and colour. Jess, Lil, Mary, Blue and Molly were all squashed into the back seat of the taxi. People in cars honked and hooted and waved at them as they went by. It was the best day of the whole year – the day the Dublin taxi drivers took the children from the city's orphanages on a special day out. And it was the start of summer.

'Are you all right in the back there?' called Jimmy Mooney.

'Yeah, yeah, yeah!' they screamed back.

They'd been up since early morning, and they'd said prayers at mass for the sun to shine and the rain to stay away. There had been no complaints at breakfast about lumpy or cold porridge or sour milk or no sugar, as nobody wanted to start the day with complaining. Even the nuns and kitchen staff were smiling – for once they too were having a day off and getting rid of their charges for a few hours.

'The weather forecast is good,' beamed Mrs MacFadden, the cook, as Blue pushed the heavy trolley of empty bowls and cups back into the kitchen.

'Really?'

'Aye, dry spells and sunshine, that's what the man on the radio said,' replied the cook as she began to empty the bowls into the slops bucket for the pigs.

Blue hoped that wherever they were headed it was somewhere out of doors. Every year the destination was a mystery, with no one knowing where they were going till they arrived. Last year they had gone to the pantomime in the Gaiety theatre and afterwards there had been tea and sausage rolls and cakes in a big hall nearby, and the lady who played Cinderella and the man who played Buttons had come to meet them.

She wondered where they were going this year.

Jimmy Mooney introduced the gang of friends to his mother, who was sitting in the front seat of the car.

'She's come along to help out and give me a hand with you all on the mystery tour today,' he announced, his eyes kind in his big ruddy face.

Mystery tour! They all looked at each other, almost bursting with excitement.

'Nance Mooney,' said the old woman, introducing herself. 'Humbugs, pineapple chunks or a toffee?' She turned around and offered them all a sweet from the paper bag in her plump hand. Blue chose a toffee.

Jess took the three biggest humbugs, stuffing one into her mouth and putting the other two in her pocket for later.

'Where are we going, mister?' asked Mary.

'Ah now, you wouldn't want me to ruin your surprise. There's plenty of fun and games organised for you, that's all I'll say.'

'Are we going to Kerry?' asked Jess.

'That's a bit far, pet,' he replied, 'especially with a crowd like this.'

'Are we staying in Dublin?' cajoled Lil.

'Maybe.'

'Are we going to Ringsend?' Molly called out.

'Ringsend?'

'That's where I used to live with my mammy and daddy,' she said eagerly. 'I'd like to see it.'

'I'm sorry.' Blue could see the driver's eyes soften as he looked in the mirror. 'We're not going anywhere near it, I'm afraid.'

Molly wriggled on Blue's lap and Blue gave her a hug, hoping the little girl would forget her sadness for once and just enjoy the day.

They drove through the city, crossed a bridge over the River Liffey and went up O'Connell Street, the biggest and widest street in Dublin. Jimmy pointed out Clery's famous clock, the GPO, and the Gresham hotel where all the famous film stars stayed.

'Nearly there, girls,' announced Jimmy at last as the black Ford Cortina car turned up onto a big roadway with vast green fields and woodlands on either side.

'Is this a park?'

'One of the biggest in Europe,' he grinned. 'This is the Phoenix Park. See that house over there, the big white one? That's where the President of Ireland lives.'

'Is this his garden?' Mary asked, as they all gaped out the window at the huge lawns and trees.

'No,' he laughed. 'This garden belongs to the people of Dublin, to all of us.'

He turned off another road, following a line of cars driving slowly one after another. There were kids crammed into every car, all, like themselves, anxious to discover their destination.

Minutes later they came to a halt near to a big wooden fence and a gateway with a thatched awning, and letters carved on it with the name: Dublin Zoo. Blue couldn't believe it – the very place she'd wanted to go.

They all had to form a line, and one by one pushed through the heavy iron turnstiles that signalled the entrance to the zoo. Mrs Mooney helped to count the tickets and make sure there was one for everyone.

'Bernadette O'Malley, Lily Hennessy, Molly Dempsey ...' A man with a big hat was calling out names and putting the children into groups. 'You must all stay in your group,' he warned, 'as we don't want anyone to get lost. Some of these animals are dangerous, to say the least. You are not allowed to feed the animals unless the keepers permit it, nor are you to frighten or startle the animals in any way. Do you all understand me?'

'Yes,' they all chorused, eager to get on their way and begin exploring.

Once Blue's group was organised, Jimmy and Mrs Mooney, and a short little man with sunglasses called Bill, began to lead them on a tour of the zoo.

The air all around was filled with noise, sounds so strange and different – squawks and screeches and roars and chattering, sounds of the jungles and forests – that for a second Blue was a little scared.

Molly gripped her hand tightly.

'It's all right, Molly,' she reassured the little girl. 'The animals can't hurt us.'

They stopped to gaze at deer behind a high wire fence. There were reindeer with big, heavy antlers, thin, nervous gazelles and strange animals called wildebeest, all chewing at the grass and blinking slowly at them. Along the edge of a big lake was a flock of pink flamingoes each balanced on one leg, not even wobbling as the girls from Larch Hill ran noisily past them. Blue was reminded of Sister Monica's stories of Africa, where all the animals gathered at the water hole when the sun went down.

Bill led them right to the lion's den. They don't look very fierce, thought Blue, until she noticed the hunk of meaty bone that the male lion was eating, his huge mane moving as he tossed the heavy bone back and forth like a little piece of cloth.

Beside every enclosure was a big sign with information about the animal and a map showing what part of the world it came from. Blue read each one carefully and told Molly all about the animals.

Blue wrinkled her nose when they went into the reptile house. It was much warmer here. Lizards and scaly things stuck out their tongues at them, some lizards able to hide by changing colour to look like stones and twigs.

'Look, there he is!' shouted Molly as a lizard darted out his tongue against the glass. There were slimy snakes, a sleepy boa constrictor and a huge crocodile half-hidden under dirty brown water. They could see him blink. Blue told her friends of Sister Monica's story of the great big basking crocodile that lay hidden in Lake Azura waiting for the chance to snap his jaws and grab at the arm or leg of some unwary swimmer or water carrier. He looked sleepy and rather harmless, the nun had said, but suddenly, with a flip of his tail and a twist of his heavy body he could swim and catch his victim in a few seconds.

'Yuk! Let's get out of here,' suggested Lil.

They were all glad to get back out to the sunshine and fresh air.

The tall giraffes stretched out their big, long necks to stare at the children over a high fence. Blue looked into their big, gentle eyes, wondering if they wished they were back in Africa.

Jimmy Mooney asked the elephant keeper if they could come closer to see the elephant.

'Aye, bring them along in,' he said. 'Princess won't hurt them. She's a gentle giant.'

Blue couldn't believe it when she was allowed to stroke the elephant's skin. It felt rough and hard and the elephant in return touched her with the tip of her long trunk, snuffling at her clothes with curiosity.

The keeper passed her a piece of what looked like dried-out madeira cake. 'Hold it still in the palm of your hand and Princess will find it for herself.'

Blue giggled as the elephant's trunk curved around suddenly, sniffed at her hand, the hairs tickling her, then grabbed the piece of food and passed it into her mouth. The other kids were all open-mouthed, watching.

'No, no!' said Lil, shaking her head when the keeper offered to let her have a go.

There was so much to see and do, Blue was dizzy with it all.

The sea lions chased clumsily around the rocks, barking, but moved like sleek machines once they dived in the water. The polar bear looked so hot and sad with his heavy, yellow-white coat and big paws as he paced back and forth on the grey concrete and rocks.

'Poor bear,' murmured Molly, standing in front of the railings. 'He's lonesome.'

Hot and thirsty, they all gave whoops of joy when Mrs Mooney declared that she was starving and led them into the big restaurant. From the upstairs tables they could still watch the animals and the lake below.

There were jugs of orange and lemonade ready for them, and waitresses in smart black-and-white uniforms carried out big trays laden with plates of fat sausages and crisp golden chips. It was yummy. Blue dipped her chips in the thick, red tomato sauce, trying not to burn her mouth as she stuffed herself.

Molly began to cry when she knocked her plate on the floor, expecting to be punished. But a pretty waitress simply came over and picked it up and promised she'd be back with another plate straight away.

'It's so posh,' laughed Molly, drying her tears immediately.

Afterwards there were bowls of orange jelly and ice-cream.

'Have you lot had enough yet?' Jimmy joked, patting his own big stomach. 'You've still got to see the monkeys and Pets' Corner. So hurry it up!'

They all queued up for the ladies' toilet before rushing back downstairs and out onto the grassy front lawn again. Mrs Mooney checked their names off her list and led them to where all the noise was coming from.

The monkeys screeched and jumped around their cages while the chimpanzees stretched their paws out through the bars and seemed to want to talk to the children. They reminded Blue of the babies in the nursery. She wished she could open the bars and lift one out and hold it in her arms.

Pets' Corner was the very last place on the list.

'This is the best place of all,' smiled Molly, who admitted to being scared of a lot of the animals they had already seen. Here, instead of tall wire cages and bars, there were low wooden fences and straw, and you were allowed to stroke and pet the animals.

There were pigs and goats and ducks and rabbits and baby lambs and fluffy yellow chicks that chirped and cheeped, and two old donkeys called Tilly and Tommy. The children raced between all the animals, finding it hard to choose which was their favourite.

There was also a wishing chair, like a big toadstool, and they all took a turn to sit into it and make a wish. Blue sat on the curved stone seat and closed her eyes; she wished as hard as she could that she would find a family of her own some day.

There were two play houses and a slide there too and Blue watched as Molly joined in the fun with all of the other smaller kids, her brown eyes shining. She had taken a liking to the rabbits and looked so happy when the keeper placed a soft white fluffy rabbit in her arms.

'He's lovely,' smiled Molly, stroking the rabbit's head and holding a small carrot for it to chew.

They all wished they could stay at the zoo forever, playing with animals. But finally Jimmy called the group together.

'We've got to make sure we have everybody before we leave the zoo,' said Mrs Mooney, calling out their names again.

'Aaaaahhh!' they all complained, not wanting the day to end.

'We don't want to go back to awful Larch Hill!' a brave voice called from the back. Lil and Blue agreed that it was lucky Sister Regina wasn't there.

'Now, now, the day's not over yet,' said Bill, pushing his sunglasses up on his forehead, 'no, not at all. There's going to be fun and games in the park, and a few more goodies before you all go home, I promise.'

A huge cheer greeted that announcement and they all followed Jimmy and Bill and Mrs Mooney back outside. This time they were barely sitting in Jimmy's taxi before he stopped again.

'Here you are now,' he said, throwing open the car door. Blue and Lil and Mary and Jess and Molly ran with whoops and shouts to follow all the other boys and girls who were racing down a grassy hill to an enormous hollow below. It was like a huge green bowl, surrounded by trees and grass. They could roar and scream as much as they liked, for there was nobody to tell them to hush up or be quiet as they tumbled and rolled down the grassy bank. There were races and teams and they played football too, the boys beating the girls silly. But nobody cared. When they were panting and out of breath, there was a big picnic with sandwiches, bags of crisps and lukewarm orange in paper cups. As they went back up the hill, the sun started to dip. They all agreed that it had been the best day out ever and that Mrs Mooney and Jimmy and all the taxi men and helpers had made it so.

'Three cheers for everyone,' shouted a boy with red hair and freckles who had put the knee out of his trousers and had grass stains on his grey jumper, not caring how much trouble he'd get into back at the boys' home later.

'Hip, hip, hurray!' they chorused, wanting to remember the good times they'd all shared. 'Hip, hip, hurray!'

CHAPTER 6

Getting Even

Blue tried her best each night to rouse Molly from her sleep and make her go to the toilet, but Molly would turn over and protest, not wanting to leave the cosy warmth of the bed. Blue would shake her, call her, get cross with her. Some nights it worked, but other times Blue herself was just too tired, worn out from schoolwork, kitchen work and working in the bead room making rosaries, and she fell into a deep sleep, Molly's bedwetting problems forgotten. And in the morning there wasn't enough time to help her wash without getting in trouble herself for being late for mass.

She hated the name-calling and the shaming that inevitably followed as Molly had to strip her bed, yet again, and carry the sheets to the laundry room in front of everyone. Sister Regina, the head nun, had even summoned Molly to her office for a scolding, but none of it did any good. Blue watched as the little girl became more withdrawn and isolated from the other children, ashamed of herself.

'The poor kid,' murmured Lil one lunchtime. 'I heard some of the kids in school call her Stinky, and they won't sit beside her.'

'That's so mean and cruel,' agreed Blue. 'She's been through enough with getting put in here when her mother died. It's just not fair.'

'I know, but what can anyone do about it?'

Blue racked her brains, as the taunting and jeering got worse. It was as if Joan and her friends actually *wanted* Molly to fail every morning so they would have the fun of jeering at her at the start of the day. Blue got angry even thinking about it. She had promised Sister Monica to watch her temper and try to take things slowly and gently, but she was sorely tempted to lash out. She couldn't – no, wouldn't – let them away with tormenting the little girl. She would think of something.

The idea came to her in a flash, in the middle of history class. Mrs Brady, her teacher, looked at her suspiciously, wondering why she was grinning to herself. It was so simple. She wouldn't tell Molly in case she got the child into more trouble. She would do this all on her own. There was only one thing she needed and she hoped Big Ellen would agree.

After tea and homework Blue volunteered to go up and help with the babies. Big Ellen laughed out loud when she heard what Blue wanted.

That night Blue had to stay awake. She dozed fitfully until she finally heard the nuns turn off the lights and head for their own beds. Blue woke Molly and made her go to the bathroom; then she visited the bathroom herself. She waited and waited until Molly and the rest of the dormitory were fast asleep before she sneaked over to Joan's bed, a plastic potty in her hand.

Joan's broad face was peaceful as she slept, the blanket pulled up almost over her nose. She was dead to the world.

Blue took her time and very gently worked her way around the bed, easing the blankets and sheets back ever so slowly. She mustn't wake Joan. The girl stirred in her sleep, her arm lashing out as if she sensed something, before rolling right over on her other side.

Blue held her breath, waited a few moments, then finished off what she was doing, and dropped the covers back down. Exhausted, she crept back to bed, not stirring till Sister Carmel's booming voice woke them in the morning.

'Morning, Molly!' Blue said, grinning.

Molly sat up, her look of trepidation disappearing as soon as she realised her bed was dry. But from the other side of the room there was a commotion.

Joan was standing beside her bed. The strong smell of urine hit everyone in the room.

'I'm sorry, Sister,' she protested. 'This has never happened me before, honest, it never has.'

'Wet-a-bed! Wet-a-bed!' Joan's friends began their usual taunting chorus of jeers, now directed at Joan. Joan looked utterly miserable in her damp nightdress as the nun surveyed her yellow-stained sheets and all the girls pressed forward to see what was going on.

'This is a disgrace,' shouted the nun. 'A big girl your age not having control of her bladder. I never heard the like of it. Sister Regina will have to be informed of this.'

'Please, Sister, I'm sorry, I don't know how it happened. I must have been too tired.'

Joan looked like she was about to break down and cry. 'I have to go to the bathroom.'

'Bathroom? You'll carry those sheets to the laundry room first, my girl.'

'Please, Sister, let me carry them downstairs later.'

'You will remove those filthy sheets immediately.'

Blue felt a momentary pang of guilt as Joan bundled the wet sheets in her arms, a look of utter shame on her face. But she was rewarded in seeing the rapt attention of Molly, who stood watching, her eyes bright with pride at her own dry bed.

'Wet-a-bed!' the voices from the corner came again.

Joan ran over and would have attacked her friends but for the intervention of the nun, who took her out to the busy corridor to discuss her bad behaviour.

Blue glanced around the room. Some of the girls were embarrassed, others were wondering: if it happened to Joan could it happen to me? She tried to hide her smile for she had a feeling that there would be no more jeers or name-calling, not in their dormitory at least.

CHAPTER 7

The Maguires

Blue's longing to find a family of her own continued, even after her disappointment with the Hickeys. She was sure that somewhere in the world there was someone she could love or care for who would love her right back.

Sister Gabriel was the nun in charge of placements. Blue was called to see her and when she told the nun of her wish Sister Gabriel's face filled with concern. 'You know how difficult it is to find a placement once you get older, Bernadette. All the families tend to want the same thing, a baby or a small child.'

'I know,' said Blue. But she was adamant she wanted to try and find a family of her own, no matter what.

'I really want to try again, Sister.'

The nun studied the girl in front of her with the piercing blue eyes, who seemed to have spent more time in her office over the past four years than most. A wild child, unsettled, bold, troublesome, lonely were just some of the many words she'd written on the file. Finding a family who would want to take her on would be difficult.

Sister Gabriel turned over page after page of her file.

'I do have another couple here on my list, the Maguires. Small farmers, they only recently applied for a visit. They have three children, three boys I believe.'

Three boys. Blue imagined that could be fun.

'Apparently Mrs Maguire would really like to host or foster a girl about your age for the summer, as she wants some female company.'

Blue's heart lifted. Someone who wanted a girl, wanted a girl to talk to.

'I could set up a preliminary visit with them if you want. It would be a chance for all of you to get to know each other.'

'Yes, please,' agreed Blue, keeping her fingers crossed.

Sister Gabriel arranged for the Maguires to come and meet herself and Blue at Larch Hill first.

* * *

Blue was nervous when she stepped into the parlour. She shook each of them by the hand as the nun introduced them. Mr Maguire was a small man with a big round belly and heavy cheeks, who said very little. Mrs Maguire was the total opposite, a tall thin woman with hard, tight features. Her sharp eyes scrutinised every inch of the parlour while they spoke.

Blue listened as the adults discussed her.

'What about school? Is she bright and good at school and her work?' asked the woman.

'Bernadette is an excellent student, very good at her work,' smiled Sister Gabriel. 'All her teachers over the years have said it.'

A look passed between the couple.

'What about her health?'

Blue tried to sit up straight and look the epitome of fitness and good health.

'Excellent.'

'Well, that's very good to hear,' nodded Mr Maguire. 'We wouldn't want a sickly child.'

'I believe you are an only child?' Mrs Maguire turned to Blue. 'It must be a little lonely being on your own?'

Blue felt the familiar lump in her throat, as she gave her standard reply. 'In Larch Hill we are never really on our own as there are lots of other children here. Still, it would be nice to have somebody ...'

Her words hung in the air.

She could see Mr Maguire shifting in the big armchair as Mrs Maguire smiled. 'We have three sons, you know. The boys are a great help to Ted with the farm and the animals, but having a girl about the place would be nice.'

By the end of the meeting Sister Gabriel had arranged for Blue to visit the Maguire home the following weekend and stay overnight on Saturday.

'I think you're daft,' warned Mary, as they got ready for bed that night, 'wanting to go and stay with total strangers and waste your time on them.'

'They might be nice,' Blue smiled, hopeful that it was the truth.

'I think it's fishy if they've already got three kids of their own and they're suddenly looking to foster someone.'

'They've only got boys,' she explained.

'So they want someone to dress up in pink dresses and tie bows in her hair, is that it?'

Blue hoped not. She certainly wasn't the pretty, girly type, if that's what the Maguires were expecting.

'Mind your own business, Mary Doyle, and I'll mind mine,' shouted Blue, wiping her face on a towel and banging the door of the bathroom shut behind her.

* * *

Mr Maguire collected her on Saturday morning in a rather battered-looking Ford Anglia. Sister Gabriel had told her the family ran a small dairy just outside the city. Blue imagined fields and animals and a big, warm farmhouse, and had to admit to slight disappointment as the car pulled up in a yard to the side of a shabby-looking house, in sore need of painting, and a ramshackle collection of outhouses where the cows were kept. The yard was muddy and dirty and everything seemed to smell. She wrinkled her nose.

'Animals and farms smell,' remarked Mr Maguire. 'You'd best get used to it.'

She followed him into a narrow hallway. Mr Maguire took her coat and hung it on the mahogany coat-stand. Blue caught a glimpse of herself in the mirror, her face pale and nervous, her eyes anxious, her hair looking straggly and unkempt despite her best efforts to look neat and tidy. Mrs Maguire suddenly appeared and politely welcomed her, leading the way into the front sitting room. The air smelled of stale cigarette smoke and everything from the large couch and armchairs to the floral-patterned carpets and curtains seemed to be coated in a dim layer of smoky brownness.

'Sit down, Bernadette, and make yourself comfortable. You are most welcome to our home.' The woman smiled.

Blue shifted on the couch. There was an awkward pause, nobody knowing what to say.

'I've just made a pot of tea and some scones,' said Mrs Maguire, disappearing into the kitchen. 'We could all do with a cup, I'm sure.'

Blue followed her, offering to help. The kitchen was small and poky compared to Larch Hill. There was a gas cooker and a fridge and a row of blue-painted presses along one wall. There was a narrow formica table where, obviously, the family normally dined. Mrs Maguire lit a cigarette, the smoke seeming to calm her as she pointed out where things were and filled a jug with milk.

'You can take that in now, like a good girl.'

Blue placed the tray on the coffee table, leaving space for Mrs Maguire to bring the teapot.

The tea was strong, the scones warm and delicious and Mrs Maguire's thin face lit up with appreciation at Blue's praise.

'I'll give you some to take back to Larch Hill,' she promised.

Blue hoped that there would be a few cherry ones.

'Where are the boys?' asked Blue.

'Frank and Dermot are out playing football and won't be home for another hour or two at least, and Paddy is outside somewhere, playing,' laughed their mother. 'Boys will be boys. They are never around when you need them.'

After a while Mrs Maguire decided to show Blue the rest of the house. There was a small scullery behind the kitchen and a dark, narrow room, which held a long mahogany table and six chairs.

'We hardly use this room,' explained Mrs Maguire.

Blue had already guessed that, by the musty smell and the boxes stacked in the four corners.

Upstairs there were four bedrooms and a bathroom.

'This is your room.' Mrs Maguire opened the door to the smallest bedroom. It barely held the narrow bed and heavy, oak wardrobe. There was a green sateen quilt on the bed and heavy brown and beige curtains, which almost covered the small window that overlooked the farmyard. The room was filled with the smell from the yard. Any hopes of Mary's pink girly bedroom were immediately dashed and Blue swallowed hard, trying to imagine herself sleeping in the lonely bed in that awful room.

'I was trying to air it before you came,' the woman apologised, pulling the window closed. 'You can hang your clothes up here.'

Blue felt ashamed when she saw the hangers dangling in the empty space, wishing she had some nice things to hang up instead of the single bottle-green jumper and some tatty, faded underwear.

When they got back downstairs, the Maguires' ten-year-old son Paddy had appeared, and he was busy polishing off two buttered scones. He stared blankly up at her.

'Paddy, be a good boy and show Bernadette the cows,' prompted his mother.

Blue was glad to get outside in the fresh air and followed the boy across the yard, trying not to step in dirt and dung in her good black shoes.

He climbed up on a gate, pointing as he told her the names of some of their small dairy herd. The cows mooed balefully at them.

'Are you coming to live with us?' he asked, unnerving her.

'I don't know yet.' She shrugged.

He made no other comment and asked no other question of her, which she thought was a bit strange, as he showed her how to pat the cows' heads and give them a handful of straw to eat. Over at the far end of the yard there was a pigsty with a large sow and eight pink piglets, all running and squirming and trying to climb up on their mother.

Blue thought the baby pigs were the cutest animals she had ever seen as they squealed and pushed against each other.

'What are they called?'

'They've got no names.'

Blue reached out towards a small piglet, who tottered over to her searching for food, the little wet snout twitching at her fingers.

'He's so sweet.'

'It's a she.'

'Well, she's beautiful … she should be called Bonnie.'

Patrick laughed.

Blue thought of the fun she could have naming all the piglets.

Mrs Maguire was in the kitchen and was in the middle of cutting up meat for a stew when she went back inside.

'Can I help?' she offered.

Mrs Maguire gave a huge grin. 'In a month of Sundays the boys would never lift a finger to help me in the kitchen,' she exclaimed, 'and here you are only a minute in the place and you know what's needed. You chop up those carrots there and I'll do the onions.'

Work was something everyone in Larch Hill was well used to. By the time Blue had finished Mrs Maguire was sitting at the kitchen table lighting up another cigarette from the red Carroll's Number One packet.

'Don't ever start smoking, dear, for 'tis the very divil to give up,' the woman cautioned, taking a huge drag of the cigarette.

Blue watched, fascinated, as she smoked one cigarette, then another, stubbing them out in an old cockle shell that she used as an ashtray. Mrs Maguire talked a lot about the boys and Blue was more than curious to meet the other two. From what she could gather, nothing was too much for the Maguire boys as far as their mother was concerned.

She was in the middle of peeling potatoes for the dinner when the eldest boy, Frank, trooped into the kitchen, the mud from his boots falling on the floor. He was about seventeen years old, tall and heavy-set, with a thatch of red hair and a freckled face.

'Mam, can you give us a hand outside?' he said, ignoring Blue. 'The milking buckets all need cleaning.'

'I'm busy here,' she responded, 'but maybe Bernadette might be able to.'

Blue felt suddenly shy when the older boy looked at her. He said a gruff hello and then gestured for her to follow him back outside.

'She needs boots,' called Mrs Maguire, glancing at the mud and dirt already encrusted on her black shoes.

'Put on your boots,' ordered Frank.

'I don't have any,' replied Blue, embarrassed.

'No wellie boots!' he said, clearly astounded.

'Grab her a pair from the cupboard under the stairs. Those old ones of Dermot's might fit her,' suggested his mother.

Frank passed her a pair of black wellington boots, which Blue pulled on. They were way too big.

'They'll do,' grinned Frank, as he pushed open the back door and stomped across the yard. She followed him, trying not to stumble as she got used to the boots which came right up over her knees.

The milking parlour was small, with room only for a few cows. In one corner stood a pile of enamel buckets.

'We'll be milking soon, so we'd best get all the buckets done,' he said.

Blue picked up a bucket, unsure of what was expected of her. To her eyes the bucket looked clean enough.

'This one seems all right,' she ventured.

'They have to be perfectly clean,' he retorted. 'There's sour milk on the bottom of that and the sides. It needs rinsing and a good scrub, else the creamery won't touch our milk and we'll get a bad name.'

'I see.'

'Da and I'll be milking soon so we'd best get a move on,' he bossed.

Outside the door of the milking shed there was a cold-water tap and Blue carried out a few of the buckets there and began to fill them. The water splashed everywhere and she was thankful now for the rubber boots.

Frank tossed her a brush and she scrubbed the bottoms and sides and rims of the buckets as hard as she could.

He stood, arms folded, watching her. 'Mind you do the rims properly,' he warned. 'The germs stay there.'

Pushing her hair back out of her eyes Blue worked, scrubbing and cleaning and washing till the buckets looked like new.

'They'll do,' smiled Frank, giving her a bit of grudging praise.

She hoped he'd offer to let her help with the milking, but instead he dismissed her, telling her, 'You'd best go inside and help my Mam.'

The ends of her sleeves were wet and the front of her skirt was damp as she went back to the house, wishing she had a change of clothes.

Mrs Maguire had finished cooking and was busy sorting out laundry. Blue found herself carrying a basket full of clothes out to the clothes line.

By the time dinner was ready, Blue was starving and exhausted. She helped pass around plates and a big bowl of floury potatoes, before getting her own meal. The beef stew was good and she ate it hungrily. Dermot, the middle boy, pushed in at the table beside her, saying nothing, his black, greasy hair hanging in a fringe over his forehead. He kept sticking his elbows in her way. Mr and Mrs Maguire chatted away to the boys about the milking and the farm and the afternoon's football match and their neighbours who had just bought a tractor. Blue smiled, listening, waiting for someone to ask her a question or an opinion, or even if she liked the food, but no one did and she passed the meal in total silence. She blinked, thinking of Mary and Lil and Jess beside her on the bench at meal times in Larch Hill.

They had cups of tea and a slice of sweet madeira cake after.

'Did you make this cake yourself, Mrs Maguire?' she finally managed to ask. Every head at the table turned towards her.

'Of course I did, dear,' she replied.

'It's just that it tastes really …'

Blue searched for the word. They never got cakes or sweet things in Larch Hill so she was not used to the lightness of the sponge or the sweetness of the taste. The nuns did not believe in treats or spoiling.

'… beautiful.'

Mrs Maguire smiled. 'Thank you, Bernadette. It's nice of you to say so.'

Paddy looked over and stuck his tongue out at her.

When they had all finished eating, Blue and Mrs Maguire cleaned and washed up as the rest of the family sat in silence and watched the small black and white TV in the sitting room. Blue felt strange and awkward. Frank disappeared off after a while to visit a friend, and shortly afterwards Mr Maguire put on his hat and coat and said he was needed down at Ryans'.

'He's off to the local,' sighed Mrs Maguire. 'Ryans own the Quarry Inn, about a mile down the road.'

The two other boys began to play cards and Blue hoped she'd be invited to join in, but the brothers ignored her, so she was left watching the television. Mrs Maguire was glued to Gay Byrne on 'The Late Late Show', but Blue quickly became bored.

By ten o'clock she was yawning and was relieved when Mrs Maguire said to her, 'You've had a long day, dear. Run off to bed and we'll see you in the morning.'

The small bedroom was chilly and damp, and Blue wished she had more than her flannel nightdress to sleep in. She washed and changed and climbed into the narrow bed. Automatically she said her night prayers, naming off her list of friends in Larch Hill and her unknown mother, then adding the Maguires' names as an afterthought. She sat up in bed wondering if Mrs Maguire would come up and say goodnight to her, but after twenty minutes or so she gave up and pulled the blankets and bedspread around her in an effort to get warm. After nearly an hour of tossing and turning she eventually slept, unused to the quiet of the room.

The next morning the family rose early and drove to Sunday mass. Blue looked around the small, grey stone parish church with its stained glass Stations of the Cross and huge statues of St Patrick and Our Lady, aware that she was the subject of much curiosity. The other church-goers looked friendly, but they were very reserved and merely nodded in her direction as a greeting.

When they got back to the farm, they all had a quick breakfast and then Mr Maguire and the boys attended the animals while Blue washed up before starting into the Sunday lunch with Mrs Maguire. She longed to go out and play in the fresh air, to run around and explore or go and see how Bonnie and the rest of the piglets were doing, but Mrs Maguire wouldn't let her off on her own.

'You've got to stay where I can keep a good eye on you, Bernadette. A good eye.'

Mr Maguire fell asleep reading the paper after their big lunch of roast mutton. His snores filled the downstairs and Blue politely tried not to laugh. At three o'clock he got out his car keys, ready to drive her back to town.

'Thank you for inviting me to your home,' said Blue. She hoped that one of the boys would come along for the ride to keep her company, but they just ignored her.

Mrs Maguire fussed about, buttoning up Blue's coat, then ran into the kitchen for a paper bag containing half a dozen scones.

'Bernadette, share them with your friends,' she offered, as they walked to the door. 'And I do hope you'll visit us again.'

Mr Maguire concentrated on driving and listening to the car radio the whole way back. He didn't say a word, and Blue just stared out the window, watching fields gradually turn into city streets again.

'Thank you,' she said politely as they pulled up in the driveway of Larch Hill.

'You're welcome, girl, welcome, if that's what the Missus wants.'

She said goodbye and clambered up the steps, waving to Mr Maguire as the car moved off.

'I'll collect you next weekend,' was all he said.

All the girls quizzed her that night about the visit. Blue sat on the bed and told them all about the cute little piglets and the cows and the three boys. She didn't bother to mention the disappointment of the shabby house and small bedroom, and the woman who smoked cigarettes one after another.

* * *

Over the next two weekends Blue found herself making up more and more stories about the family. 'I played football in the fields with the boys on Sunday, and Paddy, the youngest, was crying when it was time for me to leave and come back here,' she boasted.

The others stared at her enviously and she felt slightly ashamed of what she was doing, but she couldn't stop herself. She had the girls' attention and went on to tell even more lies about the wonderful Maguire family, making them sound almost like saints.

Blue wondered how she had got herself into such a mess. She was making up things about a family she barely knew, people she didn't really care about, about boys who were cold and mean to her, but once she had started the lies just kept getting bigger and more outrageous.

Sister Monica stopped her in the corridor after mass one Sunday to talk to her. 'Bernadette, I'm delighted to hear that you have found a good family to take you under their wing.'

Blue said nothing, not trusting herself to speak, knowing full well that Sister Monica could see right through her, those inquisitive monkey-like brown eyes searching her face and quickly getting to the truth.

CHAPTER 8

Nits

'The orphans have got lice in their hair,' Jackie Thomas told everyone in school one Wednesday morning. 'My Mammy says they must have passed them on to us.'

'Girls, will you tell Sister Carmel and Sister Agnes to check the heads of all the children in Larch Hill please,' sighed Blue's teacher, Mrs Brady, 'and that goes for everybody else in the class too.'

Blue sat at the desk, feeling ashamed, as the other girls who lived in the houses and estates near the primary school sniggered and jeered at them.

'It's not fair,' she complained to Mary and Lil at lunchtime. 'Jackie's the one with nits and now she's trying to blame us for giving them to her. I don't have lice. I know I don't.'

The message was passed on and that evening Sister Carmel inspected a few of their heads before they went to bed, using a tiny comb to search for the insects. Mary had them, and so did Jess and Lil and little Molly, the horrible creatures being passed from one to another. Sister Regina was informed, and Nurse Griffin was asked to order in bottles of special shampoo and anti-lice treatment.

'I can't understand it,' Sister Carmel declared. 'They were all treated not long ago and now they're infested again. Someone from outside must have re-introduced the creatures here.'

The girls said nothing. Sarah Murphy, a new girl who had arrived only two weeks before, blushed with embarrassment. Sarah and her sister had been placed in the institution following their alcoholic father's violent attack on their mother, who was still recovering in hospital. Poor Sarah. She was the prettiest girl they'd ever seen, with long blond hair down to her waist, a perfect, heart-shaped face and beautiful blue eyes. Tall and thin, she looked like an angel. At night she said prayers for her mother, hoping she would come and get them soon so they could be a family again. She refused to talk about her father or even mention his name.

They were all kept back from school the next morning and were instructed to line up at the basins in the washrooms so that their hair could be soaked in the de-lousing solution. It smelled awful. Sister Carmel and Sister Agnes and the nurse ignored the children's protests as they applied the stinging, rotten stuff that made them cough and their eyes water. Everyone from babies upwards had to get treated with the foul, smelly lotion that made your scalp burn.

'That should definitely knock them dead,' joked Mary. 'That smell is enough to kill anything!'

If that wasn't bad enough the nuns then combed all their heads with fine combs that tugged and pulled at their hair, to get rid of the insects and their tiny white eggs. Some of the older girls helped with the little ones, who bawled and howled and rubbed their eyes and tried to run away from the torture.

Little Tommy Doyle kicked and screamed like the other boys his age, but, somehow, Mary managed to coax him into letting her do his hair, taking the comb from Sister Agnes and getting him to sit quietly on her lap. She was like a little mother, thought Blue, the way she was constantly on the look-out for her young brother, the way she talked soothingly to him and took care of him.

'I promised my Mammy I'd look after him, and as God is my judge that's what I'll always try to do. He's the only family I have.'

They were so alike, with the same eyes and slightly flat, button noses and cheeky faces, Tommy's sticking-up hair a stronger ginger colour than his sister's. Blue wished that she had a brother or sister, someone who looked just like her.

'I don't know what I'll do when Tommy has to leave here,' Mary would say. 'How will he manage without me to keep an eye out for him?'

Every year Blue and Lil had consoled her with the fact that her brother was still too young to leave Larch Hill, but now Tommy was nearly seven and a half and growing out of his grey shorts and grey jumper. They all knew he would have to leave soon and go to a home for older boys.

Blue blinked, the lotion stinging her eyes as she watched Sister Carmel clipping the boys' hair. The boys squirmed and jiggled and were not at all cooperative.

Then Sister Agnes took the scissors and began to call the girls up.

'Sarah Murphy,' she said loudly.

Sarah went red with embarrassment as she walked up and sat in the chair.

'Please, Sister, don't touch my hair,' she begged. 'My mammy loves my hair. She brushes it every night.'

'Well, your mammy's not here and you are infested. Your hair is far too long and is covered in nits. We'd never comb them all out.'

'I'll comb it, Sister, honest I will. You can check it afterwards.'

'We have too much to be doing to attend to checking your hair. It's unhygienic.' The nun lifted the scissors.

'No!' screamed Sarah. 'Leave my hair alone. Don't cut it!' She was trying to jump up off the seat and run away, but the nun held her down.

'You will do as you're told,' Sister Agnes insisted, the scissors cutting straight through the beautiful blond hair.

There was absolute silence. Even the boys stopped their ructions as Sister Agnes snipped away, the silky lengths of hair falling to the floor. Sarah froze in shock, unable to say a word, not even blinking as her hair was cut savagely and unevenly to the level of her ears. They all watched open-mouthed. Blue stood up and stepped forward, desperately wanting to put an end to what the nun was doing.

'Bernadette O'Malley, what is it?' asked the nun, glaring at her challengingly.

Blue wished she was brave enough to kick and punch the nun and drag Sarah away from what was happening but instead she remained silent, anger burning deep inside her.

'Sit back down, you'll have your turn in a few minutes.'

At last it was over. As Sarah stood up a strange sound came from deep within her. Her little sister ran forward to hug her. As she walked towards the back of the hall Blue thought that Sarah with her chopped hair looked more beautiful than ever.

Blue combed through her own hair, then watched two tiny brown lice wriggle and squirm on the comb. Ugh! They were disgusting. She took a hanky from her pocket and dropped them onto it; a few minutes later another six had joined them. She studied their legs and heads closely, before wrapping them up carefully in the hanky.

The whole institution smelled to high heaven. In the upstairs dormitories every bed and cot had to be stripped, the sheets and pillowcases brought down to the laundry for washing and every bed remade with clean linen. The older girls made the beds for the little ones, but Blue didn't know how anyone was going to get a wink of sleep with the awful smell that was coming from their hair.

The next morning Blue made sure to get to the chapel early. She managed to get a seat in the row right behind the nuns, their heads bent in concentration and prayer. Jess looked at her, puzzled as to why she had chosen such a position when they usually tried to sit at the back. Blue knelt, head down, elbows on the wooden rail, eyes closed, praying. She only had a few minutes but, timing it perfectly, she took out her hanky to blow her nose as Sister Agnes sat up on the seat to listen to the gospel. Blue nonchalantly placed her elbows and arms on the front of the bench; then, opening the pink hanky, she saw the lice still moving. She leant forward and managed to place them gently on top of Sister Agnes's black veil, where they stayed still for a few seconds. Two of them began to make for the trace of brown hair that peeped through the white edging of the veil; the others were obviously dead and rolled down off the nun's habit and fell beneath the bench.

Blue sat up and prayed. She thought of Sarah and her little sister, and prayed that God would do the fair thing and let Sister Agnes experience a little infestation of her own.

CHAPTER 9

This Little Piggy ...

The next Saturday morning Mr Maguire collected her as usual. 'Been raining non-stop for the past three days,' he observed as they drove through Blessington. 'But looks like it's drying up nicely.'

Blue looked at the soft white clouds in the clear sky and prayed for sunny weather.

'I'll drop you off at the house and be back in a few minutes,' he muttered, driving off down the road.

She was about to knock at the front door but, realising her shoes were muddy, went around to the back door instead.

The side window was open and she could hear the hum of voices from the kitchen.

'Mammy, does the orphan girl have to come again today?' complained Paddy.

'She's here every weekend!' added Frank.

'Bernadette is a good worker,' answered their mother, 'able to cook and clean and work like a girl almost twice her age. Your father and I were lucky to discover her.'

'But why does she keep having to come and stay here?' protested the youngest boy.

'When she gets her holidays she'll be coming to stay with us for the rest of the summer and if things work out she might even come to live with us for good,' answered their mother.

'Nah!'

'No!'

'Listen, I'm not getting any younger and I need someone to give me a hand. Bernadette is happy to have a roof over her head and to be living with a respectable family who will give her a home. In return for us taking her in she will work for her keep.'

Blue swallowed hard. She knew some of the girls went to work with families or in the big hotels and guesthouses in the city when they left Larch Hill. But they were older than her and they got paid. She wasn't even thirteen yet and she was still at school. She hadn't even thought of work yet! And nobody said anything at all nice about her.

Her mind was a whirl of conflicting thoughts as she knocked, then pushed in the back door.

Mrs Maguire jumped up guiltily to greet her. 'Oh, Bernadette! I didn't hear you. You got your hair cut!'

Blue blushed, not wanting to tell her why.

'I think it's nicer longer, but I suppose it'll grow back quick enough.'

Blue tried to smile and pretend it didn't matter.

'Anyway it's good to have you here, Bernadette. There's a bit of washing to do now that it's got dry again, and I was hoping you'd give me a hand with the oven. It needs cleaning. If my back wasn't so bad I'd manage it on my own, but you know how hard it is to reach into the back of the oven when you're kneeling on the floor.'

Blue tried to hide her dismay at the greasy job awaiting her, but consoled herself that these were normal family jobs – what could you expect if you were part of a hardworking, farming family? Her hopes of freedom and fun and playing in the enticing stream at the bottom of the Maguires' field were dashed once again as she rolled up her sleeves and set to work.

Mrs Maguire came in and to check on her. She stood and watched, smoking a cigarette and leaning against the kitchen sink.

'Bernadette, I have to give it to you, dear, you're a fine little worker. Those nuns have reared you well. We're blessed with you.'

Blue grinned, wiping her forehead. Nobody had ever said before that they were blessed with her. Nobody.

'It's a grand day for the match,' Mr Maguire boomed, arriving home and coming into the kitchen.

'What time is it starting?' asked Paddy.

'Three o'clock. We'll be there in good time.'

Hope filled Blue's heart at the thought of a family outing.

'Ted and the boys are going to watch the local side play against a team from Croom in Limerick,' smiled Mrs Maguire. 'With the men out of the house it'll give us a chance to get a bit of proper cleaning done.'

Blue blinked. She wanted to go to the match too instead of being stuck here cleaning and washing. 'I'd love to see the match,' she murmured.

Mr Maguire's eyes looked puzzled, and the boys looked jealous as they all exclaimed in unison, 'No!'

'Hurling isn't for women,' Mrs Maguire explained. 'Especially not for girls like yourself.'

Blue was angry and resentful as Mrs Maguire waved the others off after lunch.

The boy's bedrooms were like pigsties. Mrs Maguire had decided, with the good early summer drying weather, to change all their beds. When the beds were stripped, Mrs Maguire told Blue to brush and then wash the lino in each bedroom. In no time the sweat was rolling off her. The only bedroom that was left untouched was her own.

'You can do that yourself another day,' suggested the woman.

Eventually the washing line was filled with top sheets and under-sheets and pillowcases, and heavy candlewick and sateen bed covers that flapped lazily in the breeze.

'I'm exhausted,' yawned Mrs Maguire. 'I think I'll put my feet up for a while to try and get my energy back.'

Blue hoped she might let her off to play for the rest of the afternoon, but again she was disappointed.

'With the sun shining in, you can really see just how dirty the insides of those bedroom windows have become. Be a good girl and give them a bit of a clean.'

This is as bad as scrub day! thought Blue as she raced through the work, barely wiping the windowpanes with a cloth and water and giving them the quickest polish ever. Finally finished, she looked in on Mrs Maguire who was fast asleep in the chair, her mouth open. Blue smirked. Now she could go outside.

The sound of the piglets in the pen attracted her and she decided to see how they were doing. Cows were nice enough she supposed, but pigs were far more interesting.

The yard was muddy and she was glad she'd slipped on Dermot's old boots. The pigs squealed a welcome, all running towards her looking for food. Even in a few weeks they had got much bigger, their pink bodies squirming around each other, curly tails in the air.

'You little pets,' she laughed, running over to them. She leaned down to scratch their backs and snouts as they all fought for attention. There was no sign of their mother.

'Where's my girl Bonnie? Where are you?'

As if understanding her words, one of the little pigs stood smelling the air, looking up at her.

She just wanted to scoop the piglets up in her arms and play with them for a few minutes. Lifting the ring around the pen gate, she let herself in. They all rushed to her curiously and she lifted them up and tickled them. She must think of names for them all, she decided, especially now they were getting bigger. She had the smallest one in her arms, scratching its belly, when she heard a loud squeal and saw the sow wake up in the corner and get to her feet.

Maybe she'd attack her for playing with her babies! Blue turned in an instant to run back out of the pigsty as the sow lumbered threateningly towards her. She rammed the gate shut behind her, realising too late that some of the piglets had squeezed past her and were out in the yard running around.

Oh my God! What would she do? Maybe she should shout to Mrs Maguire for help? No, she decided, it would be better if she could just catch them herself and pop them back in the pen. Then no one would know what had happened.

They were all around her and she moved slowly, not wanting to scare them or make them nervous. The smallest piglet was only about two feet away from her, snuffling at a piece of stale bread and some potato peelings that had fallen from the slop bucket. Blue moved in slowly, making no noise, and with a sudden swoop of her arm had the tiniest piglet caught and lifted back in the pen in a matter of seconds. The piglet looked around from side to side, perplexed by its change of location.

Blue scanned the yard. She could still see the other three. Two were making for the milking parlour, trotting quickly, perhaps lured by the smell of milk. If they got into the parlour they could destroy it. She had to try and corner them. She tiptoed after them as they zigzagged and squealed, holding their snouts high with curiosity. Blue was getting closer as they went in through the open door of the milking parlour, sniffing at one milk pail and then another. She noticed one pail with an inch of creamy milk at the bottom. She crept over, tipped it on to its side and stood back to wait. The piglets put their quivering snouts up in the air, sniffing. God, please let them come! In a flurry the two piglets ran in her direction, one heading straight for the milk, snout down. He was half in the bucket when she nabbed him. She held him firmly as he squirmed and wriggled and squealed, trying to get away from her. His sister took off, careering madly out the door and across the yard. Blue struggled to hold on to him, almost dropping him in the yard, but managed to deposit him back into the safety of the pen. Then she turned around, catching a glimpse of pig flesh over by the house. She'd never catch this one, which was trotting like a racehorse towards the kitchen door, its two ears flapping in the slight breeze.

Blue made a low, squealy, piggy sound. Confused, the piglet turned around. She approached it head-on and the pig stood, uncertain, as it contemplated which direction to turn. Blue moved closer. The piglet tried to make a quick dash for it between her legs, and Blue flung herself on the ground, almost flattening the poor animal as she reached out and grabbed hold of one of its hind legs. It fought back, ramming at her with its snout, but she held firm, wrapping her two arms around it, trying to soothe and calm the animal by talking to it. 'This little piggy went to market ... this little piggy stayed at home ...' She almost threw it back on top of the sow, who was sniffing around, searching for it. Phew! They were all back in the pig pen.

No, they weren't! Out of the corner of her eye she glimpsed a pink flash heading across the fields into the distance towards the old oak wood. Oh no! She just knew it was Bonnie. The little pig was heading for freedom. Mr and Mrs Maguire would kill her!

Blue ran like a crazy person across the fields after the piglet. But Bonnie disappeared into the shadows of the wood. Blue would have to go in after her.

She squinted in the sudden darkness. The trees were huge, taller than any she had ever seen, stretching up to the sky like giant fingers. Their trunks were gnarled and patterned, each one different from the other, hundreds of years of history etched into their barks.

She searched around for the piglet, growing more desperate by the minute. Then she heard a scuffling sound to her right. She held her breath and crept around the base of a huge tree. It was Bonnie. The piglet was snuffling eagerly at an acorn, which it tossed around before swallowing it. Blue padded softly over, not daring to breathe, trying to take it by surprise. Both of them were startled by the sudden harsh caw of a huge crow that flapped its wings noisily and flew from the branches above them. The piglet darted off once again through the undergrowth. Blue picked up a handful of acorns and shoved them in her pocket, as she patiently began to follow again.

She watched as the small pig ran hither and thither, totally lost and bewildered in this strange environment. She was losing track of time and direction as she ran after it. Eventually, tired and thirsty, she had to stop. She took out the acorns and threw them on the ground, then sat, feeling tears form behind her eyes. She almost cried with joy then the little pink body came back into view, ears cocked, snout up, as it approached the tempting pile of nuts. Ignoring Blue, it began to snuffle and eat. Blue held her breath. Warm from running, she had taken off her cardigan, and now, without making any sudden movement, she dropped it down on to the piglet before throwing herself onto the moving bundle and grabbing it.

'Caught you! Caught you, Bonnie.' She laughed aloud, struggling to hold on to the squirming piglet who squealed loudly in protest as she wrapped it tightly in the cardigan. 'Time to go home!'

The wood was darkening as the sunlight began to disappear, and she realised that Mrs Maguire would be looking for her by now. She ran as fast as she could with the piglet wrapped in her arms, her feet thumping on the mossy carpet of the wood. She dashed back through the fields, panting, her breath catching in her throat as she ran. It was so dark she could hardly see. Her clothes were torn. She was filthy, but at least she'd caught Bonnie. Her heart sank as she stepped into the yard and saw that all the lights in the house were on.

'So, you decided to come back!' Mrs Maguire stood over her, her cheeks livid with two patches of red. 'I've been out of my mind with worry. I didn't know what to do. Call the orphanage? Tell the Guards you were missing? Tell them someone stole one of our prize pigs? Ted and the boys have been searching all over for you. Where were you?'

Blue wished a hole in the ground would open up and swallow her.

'The pig escaped. I had to try and catch her, get her back. She went into the woods.'

'You never asked my permission to go off.'

'I'm sorry. You were asleep and I just wanted to catch Bonnie.'

At the mention of her name the piglet began to struggle again. She squealed and wriggled so much that Blue had difficulty keeping hold of her and lowering her into the pig pen. The big sow created a right rumpus as they were reunited.

'Totally irresponsible, that's what I'd call it, to run off and disappear and not say a word to anyone,' Mrs Maguire continued. Her hard, thin face was taut with anger, the skin stretched across her cheekbones, her blue eyes cold and glaring.

'I lost track of the time. I'm so sorry, Mrs Maguire, I didn't realise when I was chasing Bonnie how late it was or that it was getting dark and that you would be worried.'

'Bonnie!' She harrumphed. 'Tell me, how did the piglet get to be out of her pen?'

Blue gave a silent sigh of relief that she had managed to get the other three back in the pen without anyone knowing they'd escaped, but there was no escaping this time.

'I was playing with her,' she admitted honestly.

'Wait till Ted hears about this,' Mrs Maguire said tersely, turning back towards the house.

Mrs Maguire didn't soften or relent, and when the others returned she broke into a tirade against Blue, saying how ungrateful she was for their kindness.

Later that night, Blue pulled the curtains in her bedroom, shutting out the night, and lay hunched up in the bed feeling miserable. She shivered with cold as she wrapped the blanket around her shoulders. Reaching down to the floor, she pulled the yellow book from her bag. Like an old friend, its glossy cover comforted her as her fingers gently turned the pages. She slowly flipped through the pages with the tiger and her new cubs and the two men on horseback looking out over the grassy prairies, imagining the feel of the warm wind in her hair and the sensation of riding bareback, her legs dangling on a piebald pony. Moving on through the book, Blue eventually settled on the village of Omura on the shores of the River Kenga in southern Africa, the smiling face of Teza becoming hers as the cold of the bedroom disappeared. She felt the warm sun on her back, heard the laughter of the women and children around her. She stood surrounded by thatched huts, as the old blind woman warned her yet again to watch out for father crocodile when she went to fetch water from the river.

'Aye aye aye,' sang the women in Teza's ears. Blue felt the hot earth beneath her feet, the bead ankle bracelet moving as she swayed with the women of the tribe, making music as she walked.

CHAPTER 10

Trouble, Trouble

The Maguires were still mad with her the next morning and they drove to mass and back in total silence. She could feel a lump like a hard rock in her throat. She kept saying sorry but nobody listened. Nobody spoke to her either.

Mrs Maguire's mother was sick and she was worried about her.

'Harry and I are going over to see my poor mother,' she announced when they got home. 'You boys be good and take care of the place. We won't be too long.'

Paddy kicked up about having to stay home and ended up going with his parents.

'The milking is done so there's no need for anyone to disturb the animals,' Mr Maguire said, glancing over at Blue.

Blue wished she could disappear into the ground.

'There's soup and brown bread if ye're hungry and I'll put on the dinner when I get back,' added Mrs Maguire as she pulled on her coat and fetched her black leather handbag.

Blue watched the car pull out of the yard and disappear down the laneway. She felt strange and awkward. Frank ignored her and turned on the radio, tuning in to one of those boring programmes that announced the sports fixtures all over the country. There was no sign of Dermot. She didn't know what to do. She didn't dare risk going for a walk, or looking around the farm. No, it was safer to stay inside. Maybe she should just clean her bedroom? Mrs Maguire would like that. She set to immediately, stripping the bed and getting a cloth to clean and dust the whole room before she washed the floor.

By lunchtime she was starving. There was no sign of the boys doing anything about food so she turned on the cooker to heat the soup and set out the bread and some cheese. She called them when it was ready. They didn't even thank her. She struggled to make conversation with them though she knew they were being deliberately unfriendly.

'I made a right mess of things yesterday,' she confessed. 'I had to chase Bonnie all over the place.'

'Bonnie?' asked Frank.

'Bonnie – the piglet,' she sighed. 'She's so clever. If you saw the trouble I had to go to to catch her.'

'We don't go naming pigs,' interrupted Dermot.

'No, not when they're going to be sold off for fattening and butchering,' added Frank.

Blue thought of poor Bonnie. She should have let the piglet escape to the freedom of the woods after all. She should never have brought her back to the pigsty, never.

She washed up afterwards and put everything away. She had a headache and stood outside the door, gulping in the fresh air. Dermot was outside, sitting behind the outhouse wall. She wandered over, curious as to what he was doing, her eyes widening when she realised he was smoking.

'Do you want one?' he offered, as he blew smoke in the air. She immediately recognised the red and white box – his mother's favourite cigarettes.

'No thanks,' she declined, shaking her head. Smoking was something she had no interest in doing. The Maguire house reeked of stale smoke and tobacco. It clung to everything, carpets and curtains and even clothes. Her own jumper and skirt were tainted with the smell each time she visited.

'Don't be such a goody good!' he jeered.

A goody good was something she most definitely was not. 'I just don't want to,' she said firmly. 'It smells disgusting and I don't like people who smoke.'

He flushed with annoyance at her comment as she turned around and went back inside.

It was late afternoon when the parents returned. Mrs Maguire immediately went upstairs to lie down.

'Bernadette, I'll take you back to Larch Hill now,' offered her husband. 'Josie's tired and we'll have our dinner later.'

Blue felt relief wash over her. She ran upstairs to get her things. Mrs Maguire was standing at her bedroom door.

'I cleaned and tidied it and washed the floor while you were out,' Blue explained, glad that the woman had noticed.

'I was checking the bed and I found this.' Mrs Maguire was brandishing the packet of Carroll's Number One cigarettes in her hand. 'Now I know who's been stealing my cigarettes. I couldn't understand where they were disappearing to lately.'

'But I didn't take them, I swear,' said Blue

'Then who put them under your pillow hidden in your nightdress?'

'It wasn't me.' Blue wanted to shout out that it was Dermot, but she wasn't a telltale. 'I don't know,' she shrugged.

Mr Maguire was silent as they drove back into town. Blue realised there was no point in trying to explain or deny things as the family had already their minds made up about her. They wouldn't give her a second chance and somewhere deep in her heart she wasn't sure if she would give them one either. She almost jumped out of the car when they reached Larch Hill.

'I'm sorry things didn't work out,' was all Mr Maguire said gruffly before he drove away.

*　*　*

Mary, Lil, Jess and Molly sat on the bed and listened as she told them about the disasters of the weekend. Tears of laughter ran down Jess's cheeks as Blue described the trouble she had catching piglets and how they ran in all directions.

'I don't think I'll be going back to visit the Maguires,' Blue said. A wave of disappointment washed over her.

Mary gave her a big hug when she told them about Dermot Maguire and how he'd set her up with the cigarettes.

'God, who'd want a brother like that?' said Mary indignantly.

Blue supposed she was right. The boys had never been kind to her and her friends didn't know the half of all the housework she'd had to do for the family.

'They're not good enough for you, Blue. Not good enough at all,' insisted Jess.

Blue tried to put it behind her, but later that week Sister Regina called her up to her office.

'I've had a complaint, Bernadette, about your behaviour while staying at the Maguires. I believe you were careless around their farm and let valuable animals escape, that you were cheeky to the other children, but worst of all stole from the lady of the house. What have you got to say for yourself?'

'I never stole anything, Sister, honest I didn't.' Blue was furious.

'How much money did you take?'

'I told you, I didn't take anything. Her son was stealing her cigarettes but she blamed me.'

'Cigarettes?'

'Yes, Sister. Dermot Maguire was stealing his mother's cigarettes and he tried to put the blame on me. I would never smoke.'

'I see.'

'What about the animals?'

'Four piglets got out of the pen while I was playing with them, but I managed to get each and every one back in the pen. Pigs are real clever, Sister, so they need a bit of catching.'

The head nun gave a big sigh. 'I take it there'll be no more visits to the Maguires?'

Blues eyes filled with tears and she shook her head.

'Very well. I don't know what we will do with you, Bernadette. Always causing trouble. Go and join the others.'

Blue felt ashamed that she had ruined her chance of a family. That would be her last chance, surely. She was surprised when Sister Gabriel asked to see her after school that same day.

'Things often don't work out, Bernadette. You and this family were not a proper fit. I suppose with three sons there was bound to be resentment and jealousy, especially of a girl.'

'I suppose so.'

'Anyway, I will go through all my files and see if I can find somebody more suited to you –'

Blue interrupted. 'Please, Sister, I don't want to be involved with another family. I just want to stay here with my friends in Larch Hill.'

'Are you sure, Bernadette? That's a big decision, you know. You never know, the next time –'

'Yes, I'm sure.'

Sister Gabriel stared in amazement. The O'Malley child had finally given up on finding a family – that was something she had never expected.

Although she was surrounded by all the other kids in the children's home, Blue felt more alone than ever. Sometimes she even longed to be back in Maguires' cold, poky bedroom just so she could belong.

'Blue, snap out of it!' begged Jess, doing three cartwheels in a row. 'The fancy dress party is in a couple of weeks, remember.'

'Come on, Blue! Forget that stupid family. We're your family,' Mary insisted.

They were right. There was no use moping around and feeling sorry for herself. It wasn't going to change a single thing.

'Did someone say party?'

'Yes, stupid,' jeered Jess. 'The big fancy dress party – we've all got to decide what we're dressing up as.'

The Beads

Four days a week after school Blue and Lil and Mary and Jess, and all the rest of the girls their age, filed into the big workroom with the high windows and wooden floors. This was Sister Rita's domain. Row after row of heavy, wooden workbenches were laid out and the girls, under the watchful eye of Sister Rita, took their places. Each was given a basket of beads, a wire-cutter and a scissors. Then they sat down and began the task of making rosary beads.

Blue had been making rosary beads since she was nine years of age. The criterion for making the rosaries was that you had to be able to count. Maggie Donovan had told Blue that one time the nuns had tried to get the six- and seven-year-olds to do it, but they had kept making mistakes about how many beads to wire on and had strung all kinds of odd numbers together. The beads represented the events of the life of Jesus: the joyful, the sorrowful and the glorious mysteries. Five groups of ten beads, divided by one for the 'Glory be to the Father.' And then, finally, the cross on the end. People counting the rosary on their beads were bound to get confused if there was a bead too many, or not enough beads. So, reluctantly, the nuns had stopped the smaller girls working.

Blue hated making rosary beads. It was boring and humdrum and, worst of all, the wire cut her fingers. She found it twice as hard to use the wire-cutters when her fingers were already covered in nicks and cuts. One bright spark had once suggested they should wear thick, protective gloves, but Sister Rita had told them that gloves would only slow the work down and make handling the finicky little beads impossible. It was all right for the nun to say that when her hands were lily-white and uncut, thought Blue. Sometimes they made rosary sets from just plain old string or rope, which was a lot easier on the fingers and thumbs, but for the moment it was wire and beads.

Old-lady rosaries, that's what they were making this week. These blue and grey and pearl and glass beads were for old ladies who sat in churches and chapels all over Ireland saying the rosary and praying for their husbands and sons and daughters. Blue wondered if it ever crossed their minds to think of the children who made their fine rosary beads. She supposed it didn't. Larch Hill supplied beads to churches and shops all over the country and even further afield.

'You are doing God's work.' That's what Sister Rita preached to them as they slaved, mostly in silence, fitting the links together and threading on bead after bead. Blue longed to be out in the fresh air in the yard, running around, or even sitting at her desk studying or doing homework. By the time you had spent almost three hours threading beads and shaping the rosaries, your head and neck and back and wrists and fingers ached.

'Offer your discomfort to the Lord,' advised the nun, her fat face and double chins wobbling. She was sitting, as usual, in the big chair at the top of the room, reading a book, but glancing up every few minutes to check that they were working.

'I hate these stupid beads,' Blue whispered, her hands and fingers stiff and sore. The line of cracks on her thumb and forefinger from previous work had dried out and filled with yellow pus. Her fingers were never free of sores and cuts.

'Ssshh,' cautioned Lil, who was sitting beside her, and didn't believe in attracting trouble.

'Ow!' Blue jerked out of the way as a bit of metal flew up and almost caught her in the eye.

Lil was flying through her pile of beads, and had three silver crosses already positioned on the end of each.

'Hurry up, Blue, she's looking down at you!' she warned.

The last thing Blue wanted was the nun to waddle down and stand over her, watching. The last time it happened she had been made to stay behind to finish and had missed her tea; she would have gone to bed hungry except for the bits of crust Lil had managed to save for her.

'Is there a problem, Bernadette?' Sister Rita called.

'No, Sister, no. I'm flying. Thanks,' she mumbled, wishing she had the courage to go up and fling the basket of beads all over the nun's smug face. She sighed and tried to concentrate on what she was doing. Sometimes she would make up a story in her head about the person who was getting the beads. A few weeks ago they had been handed boxes of large brown and black beads. Blue had loved the smooth feel of them and imagined the priests on the missions out in Africa in the hot sun, far from home, using the rosary beads that she was making to help them work with people who worshipped different gods. Those crosses had been made of wood and silver, and were plain and simple as could be. The crosses for these rosaries were fiddly and ornate and every time she attached the cross it seemed to turn in the wrong direction, a bit like the wayward tail of a kite she once saw flying up over the high orphanage walls. She jerked and pulled at it, twisting the tiny loop of silver wire that held the cross and forcing it into a straighter position. Lil smiled over at her.

Blue sneaked a look at the others. Mary had wrinkles across her brow with concentration, and had spread the sets of beads she'd finished in a neat row. Jess was day-dreaming, but she was such a natural with her hands that she could have made a set of beads with her eyes closed. Sinead, who had only just started working on the rosaries, looked like she was about to cry; the bits of wire kept snapping in her hands and she had dropped a few beads on the floor under her bench. Maggie Roche, a big girl of fifteen, was slowly and patiently trying to show her how do it. Blue smiled over, trying to encourage her. They all knew that there was no point in crying over working with the beads because the nuns had no time for those who snivelled and were cry-babies. If anything, the nuns made things worse for them.

Blue turned her attention to her own work. One set, two sets – ignoring the stiffness and pain in her fingers she worked on. Then, quickly, she let two smooth, grey beads slip into her pocket. She was collecting beads, saving them up for a special purpose. The nuns regularly checked the beads, counting them carefully, but there were always a few that fell on the workroom floor and disappeared between the gaps in the floorboards, or that cracked or chipped and were unusable, so Blue didn't consider it stealing to take a few for herself.

Sinead gave a sudden cry and, out of the corner of her eye, Blue saw the almost-full basket of beads wobble and spill out all over the bench, beads running madly in all directions. Sinead was frantically trying to catch them as they tumbled on to the floor. Sister Rita was on her feet immediately, barking the order to them all:

'Help her, and be careful where you step!'

They all stopped working and rushed over to help. Blue managed to scoop a few into her pocket as the girls crowded around Sinead, who was bent down on the floor, her skinny arms and hands scrabbling for the tiny beads. At last they had rescued as many as they could.

Blue slipped back to her own part of the bench, a big grin on her face. She had almost enough beads now to put her plan into action.

'Girls, back to your work!' called Sister Rita. 'Sinead, you will have to stay on to finish off the set you're working on.'

'But what about my tea?' wailed Sinead.

Blue looked up. She had total sympathy for the girl. The meals in Larch Hill were hardly appetising, and they were certainly not filling, but if you missed one it meant a rumbling stomach and hunger pains till the next day.

'That will depend on your work being finished.'

Sinead's lip wobbled. Blue and the other girls stared over and gave her the thumbs-up, hoping she wouldn't give the nun the satisfaction of crying.

'Yes, Sister,' Sinead said, ramming a bead on to the wire and twisting it firmly into place, determined not to cry over the two slices of bread or the curdled scrambled egg that passed for tea.

CHAPTER 12

The Fancy Dress Party

Everyone in Larch Hill was bursting with excitement in anticipation of the annual summer fancy dress party arranged by the visiting committee every July. Blue loved dressing up and pretending to be somebody else. It was like being part of some strange game. Everyone planned their costume in secret. All through the previous week Blue hid scraps of material with her secret stash of beads. She collected bird feathers from the unlikeliest of places around the yard and garden, even tearing a little piece of her pillow to get the final few she needed, taking care to re-stitch it before Sister Carmel saw it.

On the day of the fancy dress the dormitory was crazy, everyone rushing around gathering their stuff and trying to pin or sew their outfits together.

'Blue, help me get this witch's hat to stay on my head,' begged Lil, the black-painted cardboard cone toppling over again and again, refusing to stay on her thick curls.

'I'll get some hair clips and clip it round the side,' Blue offered.

At last it stayed on, even if it was still a bit precarious.

'What are you going as, Blue?' asked Lil. But Blue wasn't ready to reveal her secret yet. She stared around the dormitory at all the others.

Mary, Jess and Sarah had obviously got together on their outfits. They shrieked with laughter as they wrapped themselves in white sheets and made ghostly wailing noise, chasing each other around the room and trying to scare people. Their eyes stared out from the scissor-cuts they'd made in the sheets they'd taken from the mending cupboard. Joan and Derval were cowboys, with waistcoats and guns made from silver paper and cardboard, and two cowboy hats they'd borrowed from Derval's brother. Joan had tied a scarf around her neck, and a big piece of rope hung from her waist like a lasso. Already she was bossing Derval around, saying that she was the sheriff.

Lil, the witch, had a voluminous black skirt, probably a nun's, that she'd borrowed from the clothes press. She had taken a brush from the broom cupboard, which was meant to be her broomstick, and found a mouldy-looking toy cat in the babies' toy box to serve as her witch's cat. Chrissy and Annie were dressed in old party frocks they'd found and were pretending to be Little Miss Muffet and Little Bo Peep, though you couldn't tell which was which.

Molly had set her heart on dressing up as a bunny rabbit and Jess and Blue had made a costume for her. Blue had cut out two long ears from a piece of old flannelette, wrapped them around a bit of wire and sellotaped them to a hair band. They had managed to find a white angora cardigan and white tights to dress her in. Lil then pinned a big, fluffy lump of cotton wool from the nursery on to Molly's bottom to make a tail. Blue drew whiskers and a nose with some black paint on her face.

'You look as cute as can be, Molly,' Blue laughed. 'Now go and practise some bunny hops.' Molly was delighted.

'Aren't you getting dressed up, Blue?' asked Sarah.

'Of course I am!' said Blue. She slipped away to the toilet. She had hidden everything she needed, far from prying eyes. Taking out her laundry bag, she began to undress and put on her outfit, running the comb through her hair and getting the small paint pot and some ink from her bag.

'What are you doing in there?' demanded Derval, the cowboy.

Blue thanked heaven for the lock on the door.

A few minutes later Lil knocked on the door.

'Blue, are you ready yet? We're all going downstairs. The music has started.'

Blue cursed herself. She wasn't anywhere near ready. This was taking so long.

'You go on with the others, Lil, I'll follow you down.'

She breathed a sigh of relief as she heard the others laughing and giggling along the corridor towards the stairs.

In the silence she busied herself, applying more colour to her arms and shoulders and chest and face. Then she opened the door and made for the sink with a square of mirrored glass above it. She began to paint her face. Already she looked so different. Pleased, she stood back to get the effect. Her hair and face and costume were exactly what she had imagined. Satisfied, she ran down the main stairs two at a time, her bare feet cold on the marble floor.

The record player belted out a selection of songs from the Bee Gees, Buddy Holly and The Animals, a huge cheer going up when The Beatles' new song came on. The room was crowded, and Blue slipped quietly in by the side door. There were pirates, nurses, a scarecrow, two angels and a selection of dolls with round, red cheeks and cupid-bow lips. Four of the older girls were dressed as Carnaby Street chicks, with painted eyelashes and short skirts and back-combed hair and pale pearl lips. They looked gorgeous. Mary had greased back Tommy's hair and darkened it with shoe polish. He held a battered pretend guitar and swung his hips like Elvis Presley. Joey, his friend, was a scarecrow, with straw stuffed into his clothes. Everyone had gone to so much trouble. Blue waved to Lil, who was busy chatting to Bernie and Teresa O'Brien; all three were dressed as witches and seemed to be forming a coven! Lil's eyes opened wide when she saw Blue's costume.

There were tables laid out with sandwiches and cake and teacups for after the parade. Blue's stomach gave a hungry lurch and she tried not to think of the food. There were at least fifteen to twenty visitors and the nuns were busy talking to them. She recognised Mrs Murphy and Mrs O'Shea, two large ladies who always brought baskets of clothes and toys to the home. Sister Regina would thank them warmly for their generous gifts, most of which never found their way into the wardrobes and linen rooms of Larch Hill. As for the toys, she had no idea where they went as they certainly were not to be found among the broken jigsaw puzzles, torn colouring books and ragged, moth-eaten teddy bears that were the only play things in the play room.

'Children, could I have your attention, please! The fancy dress parade is about to start,' announced Sister Agnes. Everyone gave a loud cheer. 'What we would like you to do is to get in a big circle and dance around the centre of the hall here and when the music stops we want you to come up in line to meet Mrs O'Shea, Mrs Murphy and

Sister Regina and the rest of the committee, who will examine your costumes and pick out the winners. There are lots of prizes.'

The room erupted in clapping and cheering.

'Afterwards there will be tea and sandwiches,' Sister Agnes said, fighting to be heard above the din of voices.

The tune of 'The Teddy Bears' Picnic' filled the room and everyone got up to dance. Blue jumped up to join her friends.

The cowboys pretended to shoot as they danced around. The scarecrow lost half his stuffing as straw fell out from his waistcoat, shirt and trousers. The dolls took jerky, clockwork steps, and Lil jumped around on her 'broom', giddy with excitement. Blue blocked out the music and pretended to hear the beat of a drum as her feet pounded the floor; she let the rhythm move through her, as she swayed back and forth.

All the visitors clapped and smiled and admired the costumes as the children went round and round again. When the music stopped, they lined up one by one to go before Sister Regina and the organising committee.

Blue was nervous waiting for her turn. She watched as Molly bravely did two or three big bunny hops for them, her tail almost falling off. She saw Lil show them her stuffed toy cat. It was getting nearer and nearer to her turn. In her head she began to hear the pounding of the skin drum. She swung her head as she stood in front of the judges, her hair decorated with beads and feathers, flying in the air, her costume of torn pieces of *chamois* leather polishing cloths sewn together with beads and feathers, her bare arms and legs and shoulders painted bronze and patterned with ancient designs, her cheeks smeared with stripes of colour.

The committee looked puzzled, so Blue gave a piercing whoop to make her appearance more realistic. The ladies almost jumped out of their skins.

'Very nice, dear,' murmured one of them.

'What exactly are you meant to be?' asked Mrs O'Shea kindly.

Blue grinned, delighted to explain. 'My name is Teza and I'm an African princess. My father is chief of our tribe. My costume is sewn from antelope skin and I wear the feathers of all the birds in the sky and the precious stones from the river bed. My face is painted because soon I will come of age.'

'A savage, that's what she is! Bernadette O' Malley, what is the meaning of this disgraceful behaviour?' interrupted Sister Regina, her eyes examining Blue with contempt. 'You look like a savage! A wild animal. How dare you appear in this state of dress in front of guests, covered in paint and feathers and, if my eyes don't deceive me, stolen beads meant for the holy rosaries!'

'But, sister, they wear feathers and beads and –'

'You are a wicked, wild child. Leave this room immediately. Go upstairs and put on some decent clothes and wash those heathen markings from your skin. I will deal with you later.'

Absolutely ashamed, Blue ran out of the room and up the stairs, her breath coming in gasps. Jess ran after her to the door.

'I think you look great,' she called. 'Don't mind Sister Regina.'

Blue just wanted to get away – away from the visitors and the party, and even from Jess. Flinging herself on her bed she gave way to a torrent of tears, wishing she lived anywhere else in the whole world but Larch Hill.

* * *

When she couldn't cry any more, Blue got up and washed the paint from her skin and took the beads and feathers from her hair. The wild child was gone and her plain, ordinary self stared back at her from the mirror.

After the party was over she was called to Sister Regina's office. The nun was talking on the phone so Blue stood in front of her desk. She looked around. She was spending so much time in this office she knew every piece of furniture and all the paintings and ornaments in it.

Her phone conversation ended, Sister Regina launched into a tirade about Blue's bad behaviour.

'Today you let down St Brigid's Home, coming to the party dressed like a savage,' she declared.

Blue defended herself. 'I thought it was a good costume.'

'How in the name of God did you get the idea of dressing in such a fashion? The other girls were content to be nurses and witches and Little Bo Peep, but *you* – you always have to be different.'

Blue stared at the carpet, not daring to say anything.

'Tell me, was it Sister Monica who put you up to this, with her tales of Africa and living in the bush? Was that it?'

'No!' shouted Blue. 'Sister Monica had nothing do with it. She didn't even know I was dressing up.' She definitely didn't want to get the old nun into trouble. She knew the head nun had little regard for Sister Monica and considered her soft in the head and far too lenient with the children.

'Then, where did this notion come from?' Sister Regina persisted.

'I just made it up.'

'Made it up? The feathers, the beads, the paint, the skins? How did you know about all that?'

'Well, I saw it in a book.'

'A book! What sort of book?'

'A geography book,' She half-fibbed, feeling her heart pounding.

'A *school* book?'

'It's a yellow book, a magazine really – it's called *National Geographic*. I like reading it and looking at the pictures.'

The nun was writing something on a pad.

'You know I have to punish you, Bernadette. Bad conduct cannot go unchecked. How many times have I had you in this office? And has it done any good? There will be no play time for you for the rest of July and since you have such a fondness for rosary beads you will spend that time helping Sister Rita in the workroom. Also, I told Mrs Nolan in housekeeping that you enjoy using polishing cloths, so she will assign you extra work.'

Blue wanted to say that it wasn't fair, but experience had taught her that any form of protest would result in even worse punishment. She had to accept it.

'What do you say?' prompted the nun.

'I'm sorry, Sister.'

'There may be some sandwiches left in the kitchen. Ask Mrs MacFadden,' ordered the nun, turning her attention to something else. 'You may go.'

Outside the nun's office four of the older girls sat, waiting nervously to go in after her. Their faces were pale, all trace of the thick black eyelashes and back-combed hair gone. Carnaby Street was no more.

There was nobody left in the hall, so Blue made her way down to the kitchen. The leftover tomato sandwiches were soggy, the egg ones smelly. Blue poured herself a glass of milk from the big silver jug on the table and sat down to eat. The cook ignored her as she cleaned up. She was in a rush home to her own family and had no time for gossiping with the institution's children.

Sister Monica appeared, her face lighting up when she saw Blue.

'Mrs MacFadden, could you warm a glass of milk or some cocoa for poor Sister Angela? She's not too well and I said I'd bring something up to her.'

'Sister, I'm in a bit of a hurry. Can you manage it yourself?' Mrs MacFadden protested, passing the nun a small saucepan from a cupboard. 'You know where the cocoa is.'

Sister Monica poured some milk into the pan and lit a ring on the large gas stove as Mrs MacFadden grabbed her bag and coat from the hook on the back door and left.

Blue kept on eating her sandwich.

'I saw you today,' said the nun, smiling at Blue. 'The beads and the feathers were marvellous.'

'Sister Regina and the rest of the ladies didn't think so.'

'Well, everybody's different, Bernadette. When you get older you'll realise that.'

'Sister Regina said I was a savage.'

Sister Monica laughed. 'Well, she would think that. Sister Regina has never had the good fortune to leave our native shores or see much beyond the walls of this convent. She has never felt the hot sun on her skin or heard the pounding of jungle drums or an elephant stampede. So it is hard for her to understand these things.'

Blue could have hugged the old nun, her wizened monkey-face wise and full of love for mankind.

'Be a good girl, now,' said Sister Monica, 'and reach up and pass me the cocoa tin from the top shelf there.'

Blue stood up and passed down the yellow and red tin.

'Perhaps I'll have one myself,' pondered the nun as she prised open the lid with a spoon. 'Would you like one too?'

Blue hesitated. She had never tasted hot cocoa before.

'Yes, please, Sister.'

She watched as the nun added more milk to the pan and then stirred in three large spoons of the chocolate-coloured powder. 'The trick is not to let it boil over.'

A few minutes later Blue was holding a large mug of the sweet, warm, chocolate drink, savouring each mouthful slowly, with Sister Monica sitting opposite her.

'Did you see the ladies' expressions when you gave them your best African whoop?' the nun laughed. 'It did my heart good to see those ladies and the rest of the sisters here jump. They didn't know what to make of you. Little Bo Peep and a bunny rabbit are much safer options for those judges.'

Somehow, sitting there, talking and laughing about it, the day didn't seem so bad after all, and Blue went to bed feeling less downhearted. Molly waited up to show her the skipping rope she had won as a prize.

CHAPTER 13

Pictures

But the next night the yellow magazine was gone. Blue searched high and low for it, even taking her mattress off the bed just in case it had slipped under it or into the bed springs. But there was no sign of it. It was gone!

'Molly, did you see my book?' she asked anxiously.

'Book?'

'My book with the yellow cover, the one I always read.'

Molly shook her head.

'Molly, I won't be cross if you borrowed it or pretended it was yours for a while once you give it back to me.' She tried to keep the panic from her voice, not wanting to make the little girl even more nervous.

'I don't have it, Blue. Honest I don't.'

'Did you see it?'

'No.'

Molly was telling the truth.

She went around the room from bed to bed asking everyone

about her *National Geographic*, desperate to ascertain which of the girls had stolen it.

'Are you sure you didn't see it?' she asked over and over again.

Even Joan and her friends seemed to have no knowledge of what had happened to her most prized possession.

'I have to find it!' she screamed at the rest of the girls. 'I need it. It's mine!'

Lil and Mary and Jess reassured her that it would definitely turn up.

Molly sat on Blue's bed, watching her get undressed. Over and over again, Blue was replaying in her mind what could have happened. Mary and Jess had asked in all the other dormitories if anyone had seen it and so far nobody admitted knowing anything about it. It was a mystery and Blue intended to solve it. She hoped that Sister Regina hadn't somehow discovered it.

'Molly, will you go and get into bed. I'm too tired to tell you a story tonight.'

'Why are you so sad?' Molly asked.

Blue pulled on her nightdress. 'That book is very special to me,' she explained.

'Why?' asked the little girl.

'Because,' Blue was getting tearful, 'because when I read my book it makes me think of different things, things you wouldn't understand yet because you're too young. I'm afraid that without the pictures, without my book, I'll forget them'

'You won't forget, silly,' teased Molly, curling up in bed. 'I never forget my mammy. I still see her in my head all the time even though she's gone to heaven.'

Blue swallowed hard. She must be the most selfish, stupid girl in the whole of Dublin, fussing over a tatty old magazine when little Molly was still grieving for her mother.

'Molly, you're such a pet. You definitely deserve a story. What about "Cinderella"?'

The little girl cuddled up close as Blue began.

In the midnight hours she closed her eyes and, just as Molly said, the pictures came. She didn't need the pages, the words, the shiny, glossy photographs. She could create the landscapes in her head. It was a sort of magic that she possessed, a magic that neither Sister Regina nor the Maguires nor anyone else could ever take from her as she left the grey walls and high ceilings behind and saw the glorious colourful pictures in her head.

CHAPTER 14

Summer Holidays

'Hooray for the summer holidays,' they all shouted as the battered green bus drove them down through the countryside. It was August and the children from Larch Hill were going to spend a week at the seaside in Wicklow.

Blue sat beside Jess and Molly on the leatherette seat, squashed against the window. Molly's face was pale and she had been sick once already.

'Travel sickness,' announced Sister Carmel, who was in charge of the expedition. She passed them a brown paper bag for Molly to be sick into.

'Poor thing,' murmured Jess.

'We'll be there soon, Molly, honest we will,' Blue told her.

An hour later the bus turned into Brittas Bay and the children began to scream and shout as some of them recognised in the distance the roof of the old convent where they would be staying.

'Sit down, children! Sit down!' ordered Sister Carmel.

The minute the bus stopped there was a mad stampede into the big convent and up the stairs, Blue and Mary and Lil and Jess racing like lunatics to get a room together. There were no big dormitories in this convent, just large, four-bedded rooms.

Blue made sure that Molly was in the room beside hers with Sarah's little sister Roisín and two others her own age. Sarah and herself agreed to share the chore of minding the smaller ones if there were any problems.

'Look out the window!' shouted Lil.

'It's the sea,' they chorused, taking in huge galps of salt air as they gazed at the deep blue of the Irish Sea.

They all unpacked as quick as lightning, then pulled out their swimming togs and put them on before grabbing towels and running down to join the throng of children out on the front lawn. Sister Carmel had been joined by Sister Paul, a nun from this seaside convent, and they were organising everyone for a walk to the beach.

'Stay in line, children! We don't want to lose anyone,' they ordered.

Blue loved the feel of the sand between her toes as she carried her shoes and walked barefoot. The sand was warm and tickled her skin. She sat down happily in the sunshine, watching the nuns organise plastic buckets and spades for the smaller ones, who were fighting over the colours.

Molly ran up to show off her red bucket and yellow spade.

'I'm going to build a big castle,' she said proudly, crouching down in the sand with a look of concentration on her face.

'This is the life,' sighed Lil. She flopped down beside Blue and they watched the waves roll in one after another along the shore, the sun warm on their bodies.

'Anyone for a paddle or a swim?' asked Sister Paul. 'I'll watch you.'

The four friends jumped up and ran down to the sea, shrieking and jumping and splashing in the freezing water.

'It's so cold!' shouted Jess, throwing herself into the waves, the others watching enviously as she swam parallel to the shore and out deeper than any of the others would dare. She was like a fish in the water.

Mary could doggy-paddle and just about keep her head above water, but she didn't like to go out of her depth; she'd had a scare in the Iveagh baths one time and was a bit nervous ever since. Blue loved the water and, once she got fully wet and used to the cold, she could float and do a few strokes. She longed to be able to swim like Jess. Lil waded out as far as her waist but refused to get down or put her head near the water.

'Go on, Lil!' they coaxed, but their friend would not budge.

'The water gets warmer once you're in, honest it does. You'll feel a hundred times better if you just lie down and swim.'

Lil just laughed and shook her head. She couldn't swim and, unlike her friends, was nervous of the water, no matter how nice it looked.

Afterwards they dried themselves in their hard towels, their arms and legs pink as they pulled on their skirts and blouses and headed back to the house for a sausage-and-mash tea.

In the dining room everyone was laughing and chatting and telling what they did. It was very different from Larch Hill. No Sister Regina or Sister Agnes to glare at you or reprimand you for a whole week! Blue looked over to the table where Sister Carmel and Sister Paul were chatting away with the other nuns from the seaside convent. She had never seen nuns laugh and talk so much. She supposed nuns needed a holiday just as much as the rest of them.

The sun shone brightly every day for the week and they went for long walks on the beach and for lots of swims. They clambered on the rocks and watched the occasional boat come in or go out. There were races on the lawn and dances at night, with Sister Paul showing them how to do the twist, her black veil almost falling off her head as she spun around. At Sunday mass all the local people complimented them on their singing and good behaviour as they filed into the small parish church.

Blue felt lazy and relaxed, her extra bead-making and cleaning duties forgotten, as she stretched in the sun and yawned with all the fresh air. At night they slept with their curtains open so they could see the moon shine on the sea, the silvery glow beckoning them to sleep.

Molly built castle after castle like some burrowing creature. She had taken to the sand in a big way.

'My daddy is a builder,' she announced.

Blue was dragged off to admire each new venture.

'This is Cinderella's castle,' Molly boasted, showing Blue the stairs where the famous glass slipper had been lost. Overnight the tide would roll in and wash away her work, but, unperturbed, Molly would go down to the beach next morning and begin again.

***

Sister Paul and Sister Carmel organised a huge treasure hunt along the beach and the surrounding area.

'The clues are everywhere,' Sister Paul told them. 'And are spread over the beach, and the dunes behind us and over towards the grassy sandbanks. There are no clues on the roadway, so you don't need to go there. Finding each clue will lead you on to the next. If you get badly stuck you may come to Sister Clare or myself for enlightenment.' She smiled. 'And the good news is that the first pair home will win a big prize. Now, all get into pairs!'

Blue grabbed hold of Jess immediately, the two of them hopping up and down, determined they were going to win. Mary and Lil began plotting and planning too.

'Are you all ready, girls?' asked Sister Paul, her face looking serious. 'Now, listen well! The first clue is: *I might save your life.*'

Everyone stood totally still for a few seconds, then they took off, running along the beach in different directions.

'It's the life preserver, the ring!' shouted Jess, racing ahead of everyone down the sand to where the white and red wooden pole held the ring and the rope, a few others following them. But they got there first.

'Quick, Jess, see what the next clue is!' said Blue.

A big piece of paper had been stuck in behind the ring.

'*I carry my house on my back but be careful or I might pinch you.*'

Blue and Jess ran up the beach away from the others, considering the clue. It could be a crab or something like that.

'What about the pool over there?' suggested Jess.

They ran towards it. There were small little crabs hiding in the seaweed and in the sand, but there was no sign of a clue. Disappointed, they looked around trying to think where else it could be.

'What about over there!' suggested Blue, pointing to the far side of the beach. 'Remember, Sister Paul took Molly and the younger kids down there the other day with their nets.'

Looking around to make sure no one was watching them, they set off. The pools were smaller, and surrounded by seaweed, but there were plenty of tiny crabs here too. Beside a piece of driftwood was a white card with another clue: 'Sailors loved me.'

What in heaven's name could that be? The sea, the waves, a boat? Giddy with excitement, the two girls chased way down to the opposite end of the beach where the wreck of an old boat lay overturned, delighted there was no sign of any of the other treasure hunters catching them up.

The new clue puzzled them totally: 'A dunce without the sea.'

They just couldn't figure it out. They sat in the sand looking around at everything.

'I've no idea what it is,' admitted Jess.

'Let's go up into the dunes,' suggested Blue. 'From there we can see everything.'

They trudged up over the warm golden sand, climbing the steep slope of the dune, the sand shifting beneath their feet.

'Hey!' said Jess, doing two cartwheels in the sand. 'You could get lost up here and no one would ever find you.'

They stretched out in the sunlight, the sand forming a wind barrier as they rested. It was magic up there, hidden from the world, safe in the long grass. Blue scanned the horizon, trying to see if anything could help jog their minds.

'I don't know what it is!' she said, annoyed. 'Dunce – sea? Where's the link? Maybe we'll have to go ask them!'

'No!' Jess was adamant they would solve it themselves.

'This hunt is going to take hours.'

'D'ye think?'

'Yeah, I can see Mary and Lil, and a whole gang of others way down the far side of the beach. They haven't even found the clue for the boat yet.'

'I'm queen of the dune,' Jess announced, surveying all before her. 'This is my dune,' she yelled.

Blue shrieked. 'I've got it, Jess. Where are we? In a dune. A D.U.N.E.! A dunce without the C! Very clever, Sister Paul!'

They scrambled over the dunes until they came across a wooden post with a card nailed onto it. The card said *Winners* in large letters. Grabbing the card, they raced back to Sister Paul.

'Well done, girls!' she congratulated them. 'You're first back.'

They sat in the sand watching as the others came back in dribs and drabs after them. Mary and Lil were disgusted. They just couldn't figure out the last clue. Sister Paul gave Blue and Jess a shell picture each and a big box of Lemons sweets, everyone clapping for the best treasure hunters.

CHAPTER 15

On the Beach

The days passed far too quickly. Lying on the sand on the beach, staring at the cloudless sky, Blue sometimes wished that she was a seagull and could spread her wide wings and fly. Her skin turned golden, her nose was covered in light brown freckles and deep inside her the tight coil that held her together loosened bit by bit.

Sometimes she watched the families on the beach, mothers and fathers who paddled and swam and built sandcastles and pretended to eat sand pies and wrapped big towels around their children and hugged them tight as they stood dripping wet; and brothers and sisters who looked alike and fought and screamed and ran and chased and tickled each other and played along the shore together. She swallowed her jealousy and envy and the constant question of her own parenthood and her hunger to know if she too had a brother or a sister who looked just like her, turning instead to Jess and Mary and Lil and Molly, a ragbag of friends who were the closest to family she would ever know.

On the last morning Sister Carmel told them to pack up their bags, as the bus would collect them in a few hours.

'Can we have one last swim, Sister?' they all begged.

Sister Carmel, her nose and cheeks sunburned, looked at the sun-drenched beach and agreed. 'But no delaying, and everyone is to clean the sand off them before they set foot on the bus or they'll be in big trouble. Understood?'

'Yes, Sister,' they shouted as they ran with togs and towels and buckets for one last swim.

The tide was in, the waves slightly choppy. A strong breeze caught their voices and blew their underwear along the sand.

'Race you!' shouted Jess, first undressed as usual and into the water ahead of them all. Blue ran after her, diving in and letting the cold water take her breath away.

Lil made a huge effort to conquer her fear and actually lay down flat in the water as Blue and Mary supported her.

'See, you can float, nearly,' cheered Mary.

Blue swam back and forth trying to savour every minute of this last precious swim, pretending she was a mermaid with a tail.

Jess had gone out further than the rest of them as usual and was diving and waving at Blue to come out and join her. Blue took a few strokes out, laughing as the waves broke over her. Suddenly she realised how far out of her depth she was. Nervous, as the tide and current caught her, she tried to keep her head out of the water as she turned and began to swim back towards the safety of the shore.

Sister Paul was blowing the whistle, calling them out of the water. Molly and the smaller kids were out, racing up and down the beach in their wet togs trying to dry off.

'Come on, Jess', Blue shouted. 'It's time to get out.' She watched as the dark head dived in under the water, and spurted out a plume of water from her mouth when she surfaced.

'No. Not yet.'

'Come on, Jess!'

Blue shivered. She'd stayed in the water too long and it was time to dry off and get warm again.

'You go. I'll be along in a minute,' Jess called. 'I wish I could stay here forever.'

Blue sighed. Everybody felt the same. Nobody wanted to go back to Dublin. She ran out of the water and wrapped her towel around herself, drying off her skin, then pulled on her clothes. The others drifted by her and up on to the road.

'Hurry on!' called Sister Paul. 'Get that girl in!' She pointed towards Jess.

Blue sat on the towel, drying her feet and legs, watching Jess cavort in the waves like a seal. She shook her towel in the wind to get all the sand off, then wrapped her wet togs in it. Blue was ready to go. But Jess still had not come in. Blue looked for the dark head, but it was nowhere to be seen. Where was Jess? Blue blinked and ran back down to the water's edge, calling her.

'Jess! Jess!'

But there was no sign of her. Perhaps she was diving under the waves? Blue watched to see where she would re-surface.

'Jess!' she yelled, her voice catching in the breeze.

The beach was almost empty. Sister Carmel had come to help Sister Paul assemble the children along the grass verge above the beach. Maybe Jess was already out of the water and was wrapped in a towel standing with the other kids waiting for her? But her clothes were still there. Blue raced up the beach, calling for her friend.

Sister Paul was gathering the last children together. Sister Carmel had gone on ahead, walking the first group back up to the convent grounds where the bus had arrived.

'Sister, did Jess come up here?'

The nun looked around quickly. 'She's not with me. Would she have gone with Sister Carmel and the others?'

Blue shook her head. 'Her clothes are still on the beach. I think she's still in the water.'

The words hung in the sunlit air. Then the nun took charge and despatched Mary to inform Sister Carmel that Jess was missing, while Lil was told to walk the other children to the convent.

Blue ran back down the beach and showed the nun where she had been sitting, her footprints still in the sand. Jess's blouse and skirt and knickers and socks and shoes were a messy, sand-covered, abandoned pile nearby. Blue pointed to where her friend had ducked and dived only minutes before, the white-topped waves rushing to the shore.

They searched and searched for Jess, but she had disappeared. She was gone. A crowd gathered, men swimming out to sea, diving down under the water, shaking their heads as they emerged. The nuns, the police, the coastguard, even some of the holidaymakers from the caravans and beach homes nearby offered to help. Some of the men put out to sea in two small dinghies, rowing back and forth, scanning the waves and shoreline for the missing child.

Blue repeated the story over and over again, telling all the people around her where she had been swimming and what a good swimmer

Jess was. Despite the hot sun blazing down on her, Blue felt cold at the dawning realisation that Jess had actually vanished, drowned, and she might never see her again. Silent, she stared up at the sand dunes, wondering if Jess was playing one last great trick on them, hiding up there, laughing. She could not believe Jess was never coming back! Jess, her best friend in the whole world ...

As it began to get dark the beach emptied. The search was finally called off until the morning. Sister Paul put her arms around Blue and took her back to the empty convent, the bus now gone.

'We must pray for her,' she said. She began to say the familiar words, Blue automatically joining in: 'Our Father, Who art in Heaven ...'

CHAPTER 16

The Secret

They never found Jess. They said she must have drowned in the currents and the high tide. That her body was probably washed out to sea. Joan and her friends wondered had the fish got her by now and eaten her bones clean, Blue wanting to punch them and break some of their own bones and teeth! No one ever saw sight or sign of Jacinta O'Reilly again. She had totally disappeared.

At night Blue cried and cried, lonesome for her best friend. She knew Jess had wanted to get away from here, but not like this. Jess wanted to go places, see things, be happy and have fun. Jess had been so full of life, always.

Mary and Lil were kind to Blue and even Sister Carmel would make a point of talking to her. At mass they all prayed for Jess.

Every time she stared at Jess's bed Blue felt the lump in her throat. Sister Carmel finally emptied the painted locker, putting Jess's few bits and pieces into a plastic bag. There was a *Bunty* comic, a half-eaten stick of rock and a few barley-sugar sweets.

'Would you like these?' the nun asked Blue.

But Blue shook her head. Mary took them instead, as Sister Carmel went off to get fresh bed-linen for whatever new girl would sleep beside Blue.

'I could move into Jess's bed,' offered Mary, 'then I'd be between you and Lil.'

Blue agreed. She didn't really care who slept beside her now that Jess was gone. Imagine, she thought, all that was left of her friend could fit into a small plastic bag. Suddenly she remembered Jess's money sock. It was where Jess stored the bits of money she managed to save over the years. But where was it?

She rooted in the locker but there was no sign of it. She lifted up the mattress – nothing there. Where would Jess have put it? She knew Jess hadn't taken it on the holiday because she remembered her taking out a ten-shilling note to bring with her.

She racked her brains. The few bits of clothes Jess owned were still folded messily in the large cupboard where all their clothes were kept – her winter skirt and jacket and uniform hanging in the wardrobe along with all the other clothes. But there was nothing in any of the pockets. Then Blue saw the shoes. Jess had the biggest feet ever, and how she had hated them! Her long skinny toes and narrow feet were crammed every day during the winter into big, heavy, lace-up black shoes. She could see them now behind all the other rows of shoes, standing side by side, the laces loosely tied together. Blue reached her hands in and pushed her fingers inside. There was something very intimate about her friend's shoes – her shape was still there, imprinted forever on them. Then Blue felt the bulge in the right shoe, in under the toe-cap. She pulled at it and eventually it came out – it was Jess's darned old money sock. Saying nothing to anybody, she slipped it into her own pocket. A few minutes later she emptied it out on her lap in the toilet, counting out the three red ten-shilling notes and a half-crown coin. Jess's safety money. Her escape money. Blue was sure Jess would want her to have it now. She said a silent thank you to Jess and wondered where she should hide it.

Back at school in September she could see the shock in the other girls' faces when they heard about what had happened to Jess. Two or three of them burst out crying. Mrs Brady, their teacher, was tearful too and told everyone to take out their work copies and write quietly for the morning about safety and obeying the rules. She blew her nose in a hanky and went to talk to the teacher next door.

School, work, nothing seemed as much fun without Jess! Blue did her best to concentrate but often found herself daydreaming.

***

One Sunday, about a month later, she was helping Sister Monica brush up the leaves near the front door of the convent when she saw a woman approaching. It was a visitor. As she drew nearer she recognised her by her grey tweed coat. It was Eileen, a distant relation of Jess's, the woman who came to take her out twice a year and gave her the money.

'Good morning, Sister,' she smiled. 'I've come to collect Jess O'Reilly and take her out for the day.'

Sister Monica looked up, her face upset, her wrinkled old hands shaking. 'Oh, my dear. Please ... please ... step inside to the parlour.'

Blue stood with the brush in her hand saying nothing.

'No, Sister,' the woman said softly. 'I'll just wait here for Jess. Please tell her to hurry along.'

Sister Monica stepped forward and caught hold of the woman's arm. 'Please, my dear, come inside and sit down for a minute.'

The visitor looked uncomfortable, but, seeing the agitation of the elderly nun, agreed to go inside.

'Blue, run and get Sister Agnes or Sister Regina if you can find them,' instructed Sister Monica. 'We'll be here in the front parlour.'

Blue dropped her brush and took off up the stairs. She'd try the chapel first, then the office, then the garden. Sometimes the nuns walked in the grounds, saying their prayers. The chapel was empty, the office locked and she was just about to run down the back stairs and out the kitchen door when she spotted Sister Regina on the upper landing, having words with Big Ellen at the door of the nursery. Obviously there was some trouble – Big Ellen looked like she was about to cry.

Blue raced up the stairs. 'Please, Sister,' she interrupted. 'Sister Monica wants you to come down to the parlour immediately to one of the visitors.'

'Oh!' the nun sighed. 'Can she not even deal with the simplest of things!'

'She says you have to come. The visitor is looking for Jess.'

Sister Regina turned around at once and made for the staircase. Big Ellen looked relieved. Blue ran after the nun, trying to keep up with her. As they approached the parlour Sister Regina told her to resume her sweeping.

In moments, the air filled with a loud wailing as the woman, obviously, was told the news about Jess. The parlour door flew open.

'But my child! My child! I trusted you to care for my child!' screamed Eileen.

'Control yourself,' urged Sister Regina.

Blue stood, appalled. The visitor in her shabby grey coat was overcome with grief. Her face was livid white, her eyes desperate. She looked like she was going to faint, just as some of the girls in the church did in the mornings.

'Please, Eileen, come back in and sit down!' soothed Sister Monica. 'You've had a terrible shock. We'll get you a glass of water.'

'I gave her into your protection and look what has happened!'

Blue couldn't believe it. She suddenly realised that the woman standing in front of her was no ordinary visitor, no distant relative. She was Jess's mother. She had to be. She could see it in her eyes, hear it in her voice. The woman was distraught.

Blue scrunched up her face trying not to cry too. It was too awful. Jess had never known that Eileen was her mother. Why had no one ever told her? Why had they all kept it a secret from her? All those years Jess thought she had no mother and that Eileen was just being charitable coming to see her once or twice a year. All those wasted years.

'Bernadette, run to the kitchen and get a glass of water,' said Sister Monica, her face filled with concern and pity.

'I should never have put my baby into this place,' sobbed the woman. 'I should have taken her out of Larch Hill.'

'Eileen, you did what was best,' murmured Sister Monica, patting her arm. 'You weren't able to provide for her. The child had friends here, was doing well in school. Jess was so clever and bright, God rest her.'

'Jess was well taken care of here,' said Sister Regina, her expression hard. 'But, I'm afraid she was wild and wilful, often disobeyed the rules …'

Blue ran to the kitchen and filled a glass with cold water from the tap. She was careful not to spill it as she returned. She stared at Jess's mother, she couldn't help herself. Sister Monica had managed to get the woman back indoors to sit down. Eileen took a few sips.

'You will have to excuse me,' Sister Regina said. 'I must attend to a matter in the nursery. My prayers are with you in these troubled times, Eileen.'

'I don't want your prayers, Sister,' replied Eileen angrily, standing up again. 'I should never have listened to your promises about my child having a better start and being well cared for here!' She moved towards the front door, obviously anxious to get away from the nuns.

'If there is any word from the authorities I promise we will get in touch with you,' said Sister Monica, trying to comfort her.

Blue stood like a statue. not knowing what to say. She watched the lonely figure walk back down the convent driveway through the fallen leaves towards the gate.

* * *

Blue could not get what had happened out of her mind. She kept thinking about Jess and her mother. If only Jess had known who Eileen was, how different things might have been. Maybe she had a mother too? What if somewhere out there was the woman who had given birth to her? Maybe she looked like her or talked like her or had the same blue eyes? Sister Regina and the nuns knew but they wouldn't tell her. Blue was determined somehow or other to find out the truth about her mother, and who she really was.

CHAPTER 17

The Keys

'Do you think about Jess?' asked Lil, her head bent, a look of concentration on her thin face as she sewed a rip in a white cotton blouse.

How could she explain how she felt? Blue knew she would never forget Jess, no matter how long she lived.

'She was my best friend,' was all she said.

'I miss her too,' Lil sighed, cutting a piece of thread with her teeth.

The two of them had been assigned to laundry duty, a job Blue absolutely detested. The warm autumn weather taunted them while they were stuck in the stuffy laundry room for hours, sorting and folding clean, dry clothes, matching socks, re-fixing loose buttons. Lil liked sewing and was good at mending while Blue kept pricking herself with the needle and could barely sew on a button.

'It's not fair, us stuck up here,' she complained. 'We should be outside, playing in the yard.'

Lil just shrugged her shoulders and kept on sewing. The work had to be done and somebody had to do it.

Blue stood over by the narrow window and noticed the sky suddenly blacken as a heavy shower of rain begin to fall. It was a huge downpour.

'Quick, Lil, help me close the window before we're drowned.'

They pulled the window closed and watched a stampede from the yard down below as the girls all ran in screaming from the lashing rain. Even the nuns were running to get out of it, their heavy habits and veils soaked.

Fifteen minutes later Sister Carmel pushed her way into the laundry room and hung two wet habits on the large drying frame.

'Poor Sister Regina and Sister Agnes are drenched to the skin,' she explained. 'Leave those clothes to dry there overnight. I'm going to run baths for them.'

She spread the two habits on the wooden drying bars and hoisted them up overhead. Not bothering to check the girls' work, she rushed out of the room.

Lil kept on sewing. Glancing upwards, Blue could hardly believe her good fortune. Above them, almost hidden in the dripping black material, she spotted the glint of silver keys. The keys to the office! It was exactly the opportunity she had been waiting for. Immediately she grabbed the pulley and began to lower the frame.

'What are you doing?'

'The keys, Lil! Look, The Crow has left her keys.'

'What do you want her keys for?' asked Lil, appalled.

'This is my chance, my only chance to get into her office and find my file. There's nobody around. You heard what Sister Carmel said, they're going to be out of the way.'

They all knew Sister Regina guarded her office like a fortress, the silver keys always attached to the narrow leather belt she wore strung around her waist, hidden in the folds of her long black habit. With her beady eyes and sharp face, she had earned her nickname. She constantly watched everything that happened. The orphanage was her domain and she made sure that everybody knew it and that nobody dared to cross her. Even the other nuns bowed and scraped and were ill at ease when she was around.

Sister Regina had ignored Blue's constant requests for information about her parents and her family.

'We've told you time and time again that your mother was a poor country girl who handed you into our care, child. There's nothing more to be said on the matter,' was all the nun would say.

Now, the actual key to so many questions was lying in the palm of her hand. Blue just had to use it.

'Come on, Lil. You've got to help me. I must find out about my mother. I don't want to be like Jess.' She had told Lil all about Eileen.

Lil's face paled, her brown eyes nervous and scared. 'You'll get caught. You know she'll catch you. '

'She won't,' insisted Blue. 'We have the keys and all I have to do is slip into her office. No one will know.'

Blue stood up, abandoning her sewing on the bench.

'Oh, God!' said Lil, who hated getting into trouble.

'Come on, hurry up.'

The narrow corridor was quiet, the rest of the house busy at other things. Outside the office door Blue took the keys from her pocket, trying to guess which one would fit. The first, the second; no, they didn't fit.

'Oh Heavenly Mother pray for us, we'll be caught,' murmured Lil, all agitated and upset.

'Will you shush up or someone will hear you,' hissed Blue, trying another key.

This time it fitted. It was a bit stiff, but she managed to turn it and the door opened.

'Come on, Lil.'

'I can't do it, Blue. I just can't.'

Blue could tell her friend was petrified. She looked like she was about to faint or get sick.

'Then stand guard outside,' she ordered. 'If she comes – sing, whistle, knock on the wall.'

'I'll warn you,' assured Lil loyally.

Blue closed the door behind her. She knew the room well. How often had she stood in front of the mahogany desk, knees quaking, in trouble yet again with the head nun? She knew the swirls and colours and pattern of the rug on the floor from staring at it so often, trying to concentrate on it rather than the accusing eyes of her tormentor who was handing out another punishment or delivering another lecture to her on her behaviour. This time the carved chair was empty and the room still. A pile of letters and paperwork covered the desk. She turned towards the grey filing cabinet in the corner. That was where the documents were kept. She'd seen the nun getting her file out of it often enough. She grabbed the handle of the top drawer. It wouldn't budge. None of the drawers would. Then she noticed the tiny lock up in the right hand corner of the cabinet. There had to be a key for it somewhere. Maybe it would be on the desk? She'd have to disturb everything to find it. She was just about to move the letters when she remembered the key ring. There was a tiny silver key on it, too small for a door, but maybe it would fit the cabinet? She turned it gently and felt the cabinet unlock.

Everything was filed alphabetically. She was in here somewhere. O … O'Brien, O'Connor, O'Hara, then she found it: O'Malley. Her name. She pulled out the brown cardboard file. Bernadette Lourdes Una O'Malley was written across the top of it. There were pages of it. She began to leaf through it. Vaccination record. Health record. School Attendance record. Family – where was the family bit, the bit she wanted? Then she saw it: mother's name. Her breath froze in her throat, just wanting to see it. Then the shock and utter disbelief at the words:

Mother's name: unknown.

There must be some mistake. The Crow had hidden it from her.

She scanned the page up and down.

Family address: unknown.

Home address: unknown.

Place of birth: unknown.

Contact address: unknown.

Blue sat down at the desk, pulling the chair up as she ran her fingers along the line of print. There had to be some mistake. Maybe the nun put this kind of thing deliberately in the file to prevent the children finding out who they were? She grabbed another file from the cabinet. Anne O'Hara's. She searched it.

Place of birth: the Rotunda Hospital, Dublin.

Mother's name: Jean, unmarried.

There was even a family address.

Blue swallowed hard. She pushed Anne's file aside and spread out her own one. Midway through it she found pieces of newspaper. She opened them. It was a newspaper story from twelve, almost thirteen, years ago, about a baby found in a disused building. Checking the date at the top of the *Evening Press*, she realised that it was her own birthday.

She read the headlines over again, about an abandoned baby suffering from exposure found wrapped in a blue blanket in an empty building.

She shook her head, not wanting to believe the awful story. This was not what she'd expected. She blinked back the tears as she studied the photo of the Garda sergeant who had found her. She had wanted the truth and now here it was, the truth of who she really was.

There were other clippings: a medical report from the children's hospital, the search for the unidentified mother. There was no mother found, the clippings made that clear. There was no family to discover. She had been abandoned. She was a nobody. A nothing!

She sat at the desk for what seemed like hours, not moving, not believing what was in front of her. Then she heard it from far off – the bell for tea. She felt tired, as if all the energy and life had drained out of her. She was too weak even to stand up and move.

'Blue!' The voice disturbed her.

She remembered Lil, standing outside waiting for her. She got up slowly and took her file and placed it back in the exact same spot. She had promised Lil she would check if there was an address for her mother. She searched and found the name Hennessy.

Mother resettled in London. It gave an address.

Signed away right to children and does not want any contact.

She pushed the file back. Closing the cabinet, she locked it and made her way to the door and out to the corridor, remembering to turn the key behind her.

'Well?' asked Lil, full of curiosity. 'Did you find it?'

'I found it.'

'Well, go on, what was in it?'

'Not much. About school, here, but not much else!'

'What about your family, your mother? It must have said something?'

'Unknown. Mother unknown. That's all it said.'

'No name, address? Nothing?'

She shook her head slowly. 'Nothing.'

'I'm so sorry, Blue,' said Lil, squeezing her hand, 'it was just a waste of time then!'

'Yep.'

'Did you get any chance to see was there anything about me, my family?'

'I checked your file, Lily, but it had no address for your mother,' lied Blue. 'It just said unknown.'

'I wasn't really expecting anything,' admitted Lil. 'Honest, I wasn't.'

'Come on, I'd better get the keys back before the old Crow discovers they're missing. Let's go down to tea.'

They had just turned into the laundry when they were greeted by the sight of Sister Carmel waiting for them. She held Sister Regina's black habit in her hand.

'Sister Regina has mislaid her keys. Have you seen them?'

Lil flushed as red as a tomato, her eyes jumping guiltily towards Blue.

Blue cursed herself, wishing she had never made the mistake of touching the stupid keys. They were in her hand. She could feel them.

'I found them, Sister,' she lied. 'I was going to give them back to Sister Regina but I couldn't find her. They must have fallen out of her pocket on to the ground here, near the basket of mending.'

Sister Carmel looked relieved. 'I'm sure she'll be glad to get them back.'

'Phew!' gasped Lil and Blue in unison as the nun disappeared out into the corridor.

CHAPTER 18

The Punishment

They had just gone upstairs that night and were about to get ready for bed when Sister Carmel called them.

'Sister Regina wants the two of you in her office immediately.'

Lil looked scared and Blue got a sinking feeling in her stomach. They walked down the big stairs slowly, too frightened to say a word to each other, Blue terrified that her friend would blurt out what she had done.

She knocked on the door.

'Enter.' Sister Regina was sitting at her desk, a fire blazing in the grate of her study.

'Do you know why I have called the two of you here tonight?' she asked.

They both shook their heads.

'I think you both know why already.' Her mouth turned up, in a pretend smile, her small teeth like sharp fangs.

Lil gave a gasp.

'Some thieves broke into my study today.' The nun raised her voice. 'Trespassed in my room, and hoped I wouldn't discover it.'

Blue swallowed hard. Perhaps she was just fishing, trying to push them to tell her something she didn't really know. She prayed that Lil would keep quiet and not say a word.

'Look what I found on the floor!' She pushed a piece of paper across the desk.

Lil stared at it blankly, but Blue let out a shuddering breath. It was the photo from the newspaper of the Garda sergeant. It must have fallen out of her file.

'Lil has nothing to do with it,' she owned up, her voice saying the words. 'I was the one who came into your study, not her. She had absolutely nothing to do with it.'

Lil cast Blue a look of utter gratitude as the nun sent her out of the room.

Blue stood there, fear like a huge wave washing over her as Sister Regina took the long leather strap from her sleeve. 'Always in trouble! Any time there is boldness or mischief, *you* are involved. Always the rule breaker! What did you try to steal this time?'

'I'm not a thief,' Blue protested. 'I didn't steal anything, I swear, Sister.'

The nun wouldn't listen, didn't believe her.

'I didn't take anything from your office. I just looked at my file, that's all,' she pleaded. 'It's *my* file.'

'Hold out your hands!' the nun ordered.

Blue's arms and hands and fingers began to quiver and shake, no matter how hard she tried to control them and keep them steady.

'Keep still!'

Blue was determined not to break down or cry or beg like some of the girls did. She wasn't going to give the nun the satisfaction of that. She looked down at the floor, trying to get her breath, as Sister Regina lifted the heavy leather strap and brought it down on the open palms of her hands. She almost cried out with shock but gritted her teeth as the stinging pain began.

One, two, three …

She counted the first few strokes of the leather but as the pain began to wash over her she lost track. She closed her eyes, trying to imagine she was someplace else and that her hands were not connected to her body. The magic wouldn't work, and she could feel her fingers, wrists, knuckles and skin burn as the strap kept coming down on her flesh. She opened her eyes and looked at the nun, her features twisted with temper, her normally pale cheeks flushed with the effort of using the strap. Blue caught at her arm and tried to push her away. She wasn't a thief and she wasn't going to take any more of this.

'Let go of me!' she said, shoving as hard as she could. But the nun, angrier now, grabbed hold of Blue's shoulder and thrust her forward, forcing her to bend over. Feeling dizzy, Blue stumbled towards the roasting fire and the burning grate, her skin sticking to the hot black metal; the screams came from somewhere deep inside her.

'Get up! Get up!' the nun ordered.

She stood up automatically. The pain was so bad she could barely speak. It felt like her knee was on fire. The tips of her fingers and palms of her hand were so sore she couldn't bend them.

The nun pushed her down into an armchair as Sister Carmel rushed in.

'My God, what's happened?' asked Sister Carmel.

'She's all right. She just fell.'

'Sister, I think we should call an ambulance,' urged Sister Carmel, who had bent down to look at Blue's knee.

'That won't be necessary,' replied Sister Regina icily. 'The child isn't that badly injured.'

'She has a burn,' insisted the other nun, her cheeks flaring. 'It could be second- or third-degree. The wounds will get infected. She needs to be seen at a hospital.'

Blue felt shaky and sick as the two women in black argued about her.

'I don't believe her injuries are that serious,' said the older nun.

'She is a child in our care, our responsibility. If it's a bad burn she may well be scarred. I urge you to send her for proper medical treatment.'

Blue wanted to crawl into bed and get away from both of them. She wanted to escape the pain and the strange feeling of weakness that was overwhelming her and the fear that she might throw up all over the good carpet.

'Look at her!' shouted Sister Carmel.

'Oh, very well,' the head nun gave in. 'I will phone for a taxicab to take her.'

'I'll go with her,' volunteered the younger nun, concern in her voice.

'No, Sister. You are needed here. Sister Agnes will escort her,' insisted the head nun as she began to dial a phone number.

Sister Carmel passed Blue a look of pity. They all knew that Sister Agnes, the dour-faced, middle-aged nun, was Sister Regina's lackey.

She had no feeling for the children in her care and spent most of her time in chapel praying for their souls.

Blue could scarcely remember the journey. She sat, slumped, in the back seat in the darkness, as the driver took them to the busy children's hospital. Sister Carmel had put a warm blanket around her, for no matter what Blue did she couldn't stop her teeth chattering and her body shaking. Sister Agnes remained silent and when they stepped inside the door of the brightly lit hospital went up and spoke to the porter on duty at the desk in low tones. The bench where they waited was hard and uncomfortable. Blue just wanted to lie down and sleep.

'Bernadette O'Malley,' called a voice and when Blue lifted her head, a young nurse with light blond hair and blue eyes came towards her.

Blue tried to stand up.

'Don't you move, chicken, I'll fetch a wheelchair,' said the nurse warmly.

Sister Agnes offered to accompany her but was firmly rejected by the young nurse.

'You just sit there and wait, Sister. I'll come back in a while and let you know how Bernadette is doing.' The nurse smiled as she helped Blue into the wheelchair.

Blue found herself being wheeled into a long room with lots of narrow beds divided by curtains, where doctors and nurses examined their young patients. The nurse helped her up on to the tall bed and unwrapped the blanket.

'Oh, you poor thing!' she gasped when she saw her leg and her hands. 'How in heaven's name did this happen?'

Blue said nothing, She just stared at the ceiling, feeling sick just remembering it. As if reading her mind, the nurse immediately passed her a metal bowl.

The nurse took her temperature and felt her pulse, then settled her with a few pillows and a pink towelling hospital blanket, talking to her all the time.

'You are in shock, pet, that's why you're shaky and sick. It's only normal. You've had a bad burn and the doctor needs to see it and decide on your treatment.'

Blue just nodded, not trusting herself to speak lest she broke down and cried.

'Would you like me to send in your friend, that nun that was with you, to sit and wait with you?'

Blue shook her head vigorously. The nurse stared at her.

'No!' Blue said finally, the word jumping out of her shaking lips.

'I see. Have you someone – family – a relation you'd like me to contact?'

Blue swallowed hard. 'I live at Larch Hill, the children's home. '

The nurse's face filled with pity. 'Then I'll sit with you and keep you company till the doctor's ready to examine you.'

Blue sat with the nurse, wishing the pain would go away and thinking that the nurse was the prettiest girl she'd ever seen in her life; with her blond hair and blue eyes and soft lips, she looked just like a doll.

'Bernadette!'

The nurse was calling her awake. The doctor was tall and slim, with a thin black moustache. He wore a white coat and dark, horn-rimmed glasses.

'Now, let me see what we have here,' he said, gently lifting up the blanket from her legs. Blue winced.

The doctor peered down at the swollen red skin. Bits of it were already peeling away. It hurt like hell.

'Bernadette, I'll try not to hurt you but you have a very bad burn in the area around your knee joint and upper leg. The tissue is still burning deep down and we need to irrigate it, then clean and dress it.'

Blue drew back, not wanting anyone to touch it.

'Nurse Ryan will give you an injection for the pain. Now, let me see your fingers and hands.'

Slowly she lifted her hands and opened them for him to see. Her fingers looked like swollen sausages cooking in the pan and the palms of her hands were raw and weeping.

'I see,' he said studying her hands closely. 'How in God's name did you manage to do this? Did you fall into a fire or an oven or something? What kind of accident was this?'

Blue shut her lips, too afraid to say anything. She could see Nurse Ryan shaking her head.

'Where are Bernadette's parents? I want to speak to them!' he demanded.

Blue sat on the bed, miserable and scared.

'Excuse me, sir, the child is from Larch Hill.'

A look of sympathy crossed the doctor's face. He told the nurse to give Blue something for the pain and promised he'd be back in a few minutes.

Blue closed her eyes as Nurse Ryan prepared the injection.

'Bernadette, you don't have to be scared. Honest you don't.

No one is going to get cross or blame you here. We see lots of kids with scalds and burns. Kids will be kids. Were you just messing, was that it?'

Blue felt like she was going to cry with the kindness and gentleness of the voice.

'How did you burn yourself?' the nurse continued. 'We need to know. I have to fill in this big form here. That's how we learn about things that are dangerous or cause accidents. It's part of our job here in the hospital.'

Blue couldn't say it, wouldn't say it. She was too afraid.

'It was an accident? Wasn't it?'

Blue stayed silent.

'Did someone hurt you, or harm you, Bernadette?' asked the nurse softly.

Blue could feel her throat swell up. She wanted to say how scared she'd been, to tell the truth of what really happened, but she knew in her heart she didn't dare.

The doctor came back in and pulled a chair right up close to the bed and sat down on it. Nurse Ryan fetched a trolley with bowls and basins and metal instruments.

'You look at me, Bernadette, and I'll keep hold of your hand while Doctor Lynch deals with your burns.' Her smile disappeared when she looked at the red stripes and marks of the leather strap on Blue's hands. She stroked the girl's head instead, gently brushing her hair back from her face with her fingers.

'I'll try not to hurt,' Doctor Lynch promised.

The injection was beginning to take effect and the awful pain began to recede. The doctor and nurse worked for what seemed like hours. They put creams and dressings on her leg and knee and her hands. She was kind of numb now, the pain far away.

'I'd like to admit you to a ward so we can keep an eye on you tonight,' said the doctor. 'Would that be all right?'

Blue felt a sense of panic despite Nurse Ryan's assurances that they had a space upstairs ready and waiting for her, and would give her something to make her sleep.

'I'll talk to that nun outside,' said the doctor firmly. 'Anyway, there are one or two things I want to ask her about.'

Blue wanted to jump off the bed and run away, but she felt too weak and shivery to do it. Tears welled in her eyes as he closed the curtains and left.

'Don't cry, Bernadette,' Nurse Ryan said. 'It's not your fault. You'll feel much better tomorrow when you've had a sleep and got over the shock. I promise the night nurses in the ward upstairs will take good care of you. Just ring the bell if you're in pain.'

Tears ran down Blue's face and she felt like she couldn't breathe. Sister Regina would kill her, torture her, banish her from all the friends she cared about if she told these people about her. She began to shake, wanting to tell Nurse Ryan all about what had happened, have the kind nurse hold her and protect her.

Suddenly the curtains drew back. Sister Agnes was standing there. 'I came to check on the child.'

'Bernadette is being admitted tonight, Sister. I believe Doctor Lynch explained it all to you,' said the nurse, standing up tall and looking straight at the nun.

'She's a troublesome child, clumsy and awkward,' said the old nun. 'It would be much better for everyone if I took her back to the home with me tonight. We can look after her in St Brigid's. We have an infirmary there, and the nursing assistant will be on duty tomorrow.'

'Sister, I have to follow Doctor Lynch's orders,' the girl replied firmly. 'Bernadette is his patient. She might need to be put up on fluids during the night and require more pain medication. He will want to check her during rounds tomorrow morning. I assure you she will be well taken care of in Saint Raphael's ward.'

Blue could see the warning glint in the nun's eyes. She didn't take defeat easily, but there was absolutely nothing she could do. A porter arrived to move Blue's bed upstairs.

'I'm sorry, Sister, but I have to move my patient,' said Nurse Ryan. 'I'm afraid I can't let you up to the ward as some of the children will already be asleep but you are welcome to check on Bernadette tomorrow when she will probably be discharged.'

The nun fussed and delayed for a minute or two. 'Remember, child, Sister Regina and I will see you tomorrow,' she finally said to Blue.

Blue understood the threat in her voice, and lay back on the bed, silent. She had absolutely nothing to say. Nothing.

The porter talked to her the whole way up in the lift and along the corridor, as Blue tried to take in the strange surroundings. There were boys and girls of all ages here, some in small rooms behind glass panels, others in long wards. She wondered how they had all found themselves here in the hospital. Nurses moved around getting drinks, taking temperatures and making sure everyone was settled for the night. Some of the children were already asleep. Blue was exhausted. Too tired to talk. The nurse brought her a jug of water and a glass, and helped her change into a hospital nightgown. She was really embarrassed when she asked to go to the toilet and the nurse brought a metal bed-pan. But the nurse just laughed and pulled the curtains around the bed. When she lay back on the soft pillows Blue fell fast asleep.

The next morning she forgot where she was, and couldn't believe she didn't have to jump up and wash and get ready for early-morning mass. A nurse brought her breakfast on a tray – a boiled egg and toast and a cup of milky tea. Her leg felt sore and her hands were so stiff and painful the nurse had to help her cut up her food and eat.

'Well, you sure were in the wars!' joked the nurse, helping her to get the egg out of the shell. The girl in the bed beside her looked over with curiosity. But Blue didn't bother to speak to her.

An hour or two passed and Blue drifted in and out of sleep, trying not to think of the events of the night before which, like a nightmare, kept replaying in her head. She felt safe here.

Mid-morning, Doctor Lynch arrived and Blue could hardly believe he remembered her. There were about five young doctors with him and two nurses and a heavy-set nun in a white habit, who made notes as Doctor Lynch showed them her leg and hands.

'We'll put on a clean dressing again, Bernadette, and I've prescribed some more medicine for you,' he explained. 'It will keep the pain away.'

The other doctors moved on to the bed across from her, but Doctor Lynch stayed sitting where he was.

'Bernadette, is there anything you want to tell me about your accident last night?' he urged. 'Was there anyone else involved – another girl perhaps? An adult, even?'

Blue studied the pattern on the bedspread, not knowing what to say or do.

'I can protect you only if you tell me. I am a doctor and you are my patient. What you say or tell me is confidential.'

She could see a nun in black clothes arriving at the door of the ward. How could she trust this stranger, this man, promising to protect and help her? If she said anything, Sister Regina would hear about it and have her transferred to that terrible place in Donegal. She'd never see Lil or Mary or any of her friends again. She couldn't bear it.

'You have second-degree burns, and I'm worried about the movement in your knee and fingers as the skin tightens and scars. You will have to have the dressings done every day. Your head nun has already been on to my office, reassuring me that they will take good care of you at Larch Hill, but maybe that is something I should be worried about?'

Blue glanced up. He seemed a nice man, tired but kindly. He had a smudge on his glasses and his tie was all crooked. He'd never believe her.

'Unless there is something you want to tell me, Bernadette, I'm afraid I will have to discharge you to the care of the children's home. They are your guardians.'

Blue blinked, trying not to let the tears fall, wishing she could stay here safe and cared for with the rest of the sick kids in the ward.

Doctor Lynch patted her gently and told her he'd see her downstairs in the clinic in a few days' time, when she came back for her check-up.

A nurse helped her to get washed and dressed while Sister Agnes waited.

'He's a lovely man, that Doctor Lynch,' the nurse chattered. 'He looks kind of cross, but when you get to know him he's a real pet. Both the children and the nurses here adore him. He's married with six children. Imagine!'

Blue couldn't imagine. She couldn't imagine what it must be like to have a father who loved and cared about you and wouldn't let anyone hurt or harm you.

When she was dressed and ready the nurse made her sit in the wheelchair and wheeled her down to the hospital door. Sister Agnes followed, silent. A big black taxi was parked there and she recognised Jimmy Mooney, the driver who'd taken them to the zoo, as he opened the car door and lifted Blue gently on to the back seat. He put a cushion behind her back and made her stretch her legs along the seat.

'Sister, you'll have to sit in the front with me!' he insisted, ignoring the nun's cross expression, 'and give the little girl room. You take care of yourself there in the back, love,' he called as they began to drive away.

CHAPTER 19

The Infirmary

Jimmy insisted on lifting her out of his car and carrying her all the way up the stairs to the infirmary. 'You just put your arms around me and hold on tight,' he said, lifting her easily and cradling her like a baby. 'My God! You're as light as a feather!'

Blue felt safe in his arms, her cheek resting against his rough tweed jacket. He smelled of tobacco and hair oil. He talked to her the whole time, saying that she was a brave girl.

Nurse Griffin fixed her pillows and pulled back the sheets as Jimmy lowered her down gently on to the bed as if she were a piece of precious porcelain. Her leg was stretched out and the nurse put a pillow under it.

'You take good care of yourself, kid,' Jimmy said kindly, slipping her the six remaining squares of a bar of Cadbury's chocolate that he had in his pocket, 'and get better!'

'Thank you.' She felt too tired to bite into the creamy chocolate and put it on the locker beside her bed. She'd save it for later.

* * *

Blue got bored lying in bed all day in the small infirmary, with her leg stretched out in front of her.

'Let me see how we're doing, pet,' Nurse Griffin, with her ginger hair and crooked teeth, would ask every morning as she put on a special white apron and spread a sheet on the bed while she gently soaked the dressing, then removed it and took a look at how the burns were doing.

Her skin looked disgusting, all bubbles and blisters. Blue closed her eyes, not wanting to see it as the nurse cleaned and treated the burn, then re-dressed it.

She'd pursed her lips when Blue had told her truthfully what had happened. 'The old rip! She's not fit to look after a henhouse, let alone a home full of children!' Nurse Griffin blushed red immediately, and looked around cautiously. 'Even the walls have ears in a place like this,' she remarked as she put the dressings tray away.

Blue's right hand was healing but was still stiff and sore and useless. Her left hand was a little better but she found it almost impossible to do anything with it.

'There'll be no homework or writing for you for a while. Nor stringing beads or cleaning for that matter,' Nurse Griffin consoled her.

But Blue wished that she was back in school with her friends instead of being stuck in the sick room. The girl over in the corner bed, Maria, was a real moan. She had the mumps, and her face and neck were all swollen up so that she looked like a big ball. She kept crying and saying how sick she felt, and Blue hoped that she wouldn't give the mumps to the rest of them. Beside her was a small girl called Una, with a pale face; she had pneumonia and was too tired to talk or do anything. Helen O'Connor was the only one who was a bit of fun. Although she was almost two years older than Blue, she was only half her size. She had a twisted spine and was always in and out of hospital for operations and tests.

'I like hospital and all the nurses and doctors there,' she said. 'Beats this stinking place, anyway.' She grinned, showing off a mouthful of huge buck-teeth, which, with her tiny little nose and huge eyes, made her look just like a rabbit. Blue liked her and was glad to have someone to talk to. 'Last time I got jelly and ice-cream every day and a lady used to come and give us sweets and comics,' grinned Helen, tossing her hair. 'I'll lend you a comic or two if you want. I've got *Bunty* and *Judy* and *The Beano*.'

Blue took a copy of *Bunty*, glad to have something to read.

Mary managed to sneak in at different times to say hello to her and fill her in on everything. Nurse Griffin pretended to be too busy to notice the forbidden visitor.

'Janey Mac, I can't believe what happened you!' declared Mary when she saw her. 'Is it true you kicked and hit Sister Regina and that's how you fell into the fireplace?'

'No,' protested Blue, amazed at the lies the nun was telling. 'I swear, Mary, I didn't kick her. She was the one using the leather and shouting at me. She was walloping me, and then she shoved me over so hard I got dizzy. I just remember seeing the coal and flames and feeling my skin sticking to the grate of the fire.'

'Janey!' repeated her friend. 'She's put a different story to it. She's making out you're the one to blame, that the accident was your fault.'

Tears welled up in Blue's eyes at the unfairness of it and she was surprised when Mary caught hold of her sore hand and held it.

'Don't mind her, Blue, don't cry! She's not worth it. She's nothing but an evil liar.'

Blue tried to pull herself together, blowing her nose and snuffling, not believing what a weak eejit she'd suddenly become.

'Molly keeps looking for you. She really misses you, and school's been awful,' complained Mary, changing the subject. 'We've been doing terrible sums and problems. None of us can do them. Mrs Brady keeps writing them on the blackboard but, sure, none of us can follow them at all. She keeps calling your name and asking you to come up to the board, and I have to keep reminding her that you're sick. Then she gets cross with us and gives us even more sums to do.'

'I miss it,' Blue confessed. She liked sums and problems and numbers. It was one of the things she was really good at.

'Janey, imagine missing school!' joked Mary. 'You must be mad!'

Lil crept in another day to see her, nervous as a mouse, hoping the nuns wouldn't catch her.

'Sister Regina says she has her eye on me,' she told Blue. 'What do you think she means?'

Blue shrugged. The nun was obviously trying to scare the girl, play cat and mouse with her.

'Don't mind her, Lil. She says that to everyone. She's like an old eagle keeping her eye on everything and everyone and waiting to pounce. You've nothing to be afraid of, honest you don't. I was the one who went into her office and she knows that.'

'I hate the way she watches me. I get afraid, Blue. Look what she did to you!'

'She's just a bully.'

'I should never have left you on your own in the office with her,' sighed Lil, her pretty face etched with guilt.

'Don't go blaming yourself, Lil, d'ye hear me? None of this was your fault. Sister Regina's just a bad-tempered weasel who likes to torment children. Some day she'll get her reward.'

'Do you think so?'

'I hope so,' said Blue, glad to see the look of relief on her friend's face.

'Sister Carmel let Joan Doherty move into your bed for the moment,' Lil told Blue, her face angry. 'You know what a lick Joan is. Anyway, I knew you wouldn't want her getting her hands on your things so I got this for you.' It was the darned old money-sock Blue had hidden away under the mattress.

'Thanks,' she said with relief. She was glad that Joan hadn't found her sock.

'Don't worry about the bed,' smiled Lil. 'You'll be better soon and you'll get it back.'

Blue went back to the hospital only once. Doctor Lynch was kind but distracted as he checked her knee and hands. Sister Agnes waited outside for her.

'Who's doing your dressing?' he enquired. She told him about Nurse Griffin. 'She's doing a good job.'

He made her walk and try to bend, and took each hand in his and stretched her fingers, then closed them, Blue grimacing with the sharp pain it caused.

'There's no sign of infection and the healing has started. Burns are slow, Bernadette, there's no rushing them, but you are young and healthy and will get over them. Unfortunately, there will be some scarring, which for the moment I can do nothing about.'

He disappeared outside to talk to Sister Agnes while a nurse got the tray and began to re-dress her leg. He returned minutes later and wrote a few things in her file.

'I've told Sister Agnes that I won't need to see you again unless there's a problem,' he explained, 'and hopefully there'll be no more accidents, young lady.'

Blue slipped off the high bed, the nurse helping her to pull on her coat as the doctor went off about his business.

As the days dragged on, Blue realised how much she missed the normal routine of the home. Helen had gone back to her dorm and her place was soon taken by a sickly little boy of four who kept puking in a bowl. Sister Carmel had come to see her, but Sister Regina hadn't even once appeared to check on how she was doing.

Sister Monica came to visit her most days, pulling a chair up beside the bed and making herself comfortable.

'I know you must be a bit lonely, child, so I said I'd come and keep you company for a while.'

Blue grinned, always glad to see her favourite nun. Sister Monica was so different to all the other nuns in Larch Hill. She had a heart. Blue loved to listen to her stories about growing up on a farm in Kerry.

'I don't know how you left the farm, the place you loved so much,' ventured Blue, knowing that if she had a home and a family, a place and people to love, she would never leave it.

'I got the call, child, the call to follow the Lord. So I packed up my bags and said goodbye to my parents and brothers and sisters and came to Dublin to the order's big retreat house. I lived there with lots of other young nuns like myself, all of us wanting to do the Lord's work.'

'What did you do?'

'I cooked and sewed and studied the bible and prayed all day and night for the Lord to guide me. I waited and waited. I was about to pack my bags and go back home to Kerry when I was sent to our mission in Africa.'

'I wish I could go to Africa,' sighed Blue, imagining the warmth on her skin and the strange land of Sister Monica's stories. The nun's brown eyes and wizened face always lit up when she talked of the place where she had spent so much of her life.

'They are a simple people,' she explained, 'but they always smiled and sang and listened to God's word. They had hard lives with none of the things that we in Ireland take for granted. The women of Lagira would walk a mile or more for clean water to drink or to wash their children, and gather roots and berries and grain to feed their family. They cooked on open fires just like our own ancestors did, and lived on corn meal and very little else. But, you know something? They rarely complained.'

'Where did you sleep, Sister?'

'Most of the time I slept in a hut made of mud, with a straw roof and no door. It is called a rondavel. I would watch the creepy crawlies clamber above me in the straw! Sometimes one would drop down on you when you slept and you'd wake with a fright.'

'Eeeuuk,' Blue responded, shuddering at the thought.

'One night I woke to find a big yellow snake moving along the bottom of my bed, about to slither up under my cover. I gave such a scream! I woke all the people around me who came running to help. I was such a ninny.'

'I'd have screamed too if I'd a snake in my bed,' declared Blue.

'In Africa you have to get used to these things,' smiled the nun.

Blue lay back and relaxed as Sister Monica repeated stories of the man-eating crocodile that hid in the river, the cheeky monkeys that would snatch the food from your hand, the lions and hyenas that would kill village goats, stories of children who would race each other barefoot in the dust, laughing and shouting, of how the nuns and villagers worked together to build a mission with a school and small hospital, and of Sister Monica's trips from one part of the continent to another.

Blue closed her eyes as she listened. Her mind filled with the pictures the nun's words conjured up. She imagined herself far from this cold, grey place, with its iron bars and high walls and sad children, in a land of sunshine and warmth and smiling faces.

'You sleep, child,' the kindly old nun whispered then, bending down and pulling the blanket around her shoulder. 'You rest yourself and get well.'

CHAPTER 20

Christmas

She did get well again. Nurse Griffin made her exercise, stretching and bending her leg and knee every day. When the dressings were finally taken off, the scars began to heal. She had missed weeks of school.

'I'm throwing you out of the infirmary, young lady,' laughed the nurse. 'It's high time you were back with your friends, but you must come down and let me see you every third day. No rolling in the dirt or getting mud in the scar, now! You must keep it clean! Do you understand?'

'Yes, nurse,' Blue promised.

Walking back along the corridors and up the stairs towards the dormitory, she realised how much she hated being an invalid, being enclosed and confined. But her heart sank when she opened the door and saw Joan's things on her locker and the other girl reclining on her bed.

Mary immediately stepped forward to Blue and squeezed her arm.

'Blue's back!' she said loudly, 'she's better now.'

Joan kept her head down, ignoring her.

'Are you deaf? Didn't you hear me? Blue's back and you're on her bed. She wants it back.'

Blue swallowed hard. For some bizarre reason she felt she was going to cry. All she wanted to do was climb quietly into bed and go to sleep.

'There's a bed down there.' Joan pointed to her old bed in the corner.

'She doesn't want that bed,' insisted Mary. 'She wants her own bed, her old bed back!'

The silence hung in the air. All the girls in the room stopped what they were doing and listened.

'Blue sleeps beside *me*,' insisted Molly, standing beside her. 'She's my friend and she reads me stories.'

Joan blushed. Blue guessed she would never in a million years read a story for the little girl beside her.

'Go on, Joan, shift!' said Big Ellen.

'Why should I?'

'Because we all say so,' said Big Ellen, 'that's why.'

'Go on, Jo, please let her have her old bed back,' begged Lil.

But Joan still sat there, while all of them stood around her. She was waiting for someone to grab hold of her and toss her off the bed. In the end she got up slowly, considering.

'Okay. She can have her stupid bed back. Who'd want to sleep between a bed-wetter and a cry-baby, anyway!' she said nastily.

For a second, Blue thought that Mary, Lil and Molly would attack the girl. But they held back.

'Thanks,' she murmured, grateful, throwing herself down on the soft mattress.

Disgruntled, Joan took her things from the small, shabby bedside locker and marched back down to her old bed, flinging herself on the mattress.

At school Mrs Brady made a big fuss of Blue and warned the others not to bump into her or trip her up. The other girls were curious and asked about her accident and did burns hurt. Blue pushed the pain and anger she felt to the back of her mind as she showed off her scar.

She met Sister Regina on the stairs and stared right at her. She could see the nun's face redden as they passed each other. 'I was praying for you, child,' was all she said.

* * *

Halloween passed, Mary finding the brass ring hidden in her slice of the barmbrack Mrs MacFadden had made, swearing that she would be the first married of them all. Poor Lil got the hard green pea of poverty. During November they prayed for the souls of the dead and Blue thought only of Jess as she knelt and prayed in the chapel, still not believing that the girl who'd wriggled and joked beside her and turned cartwheels in the corridors was gone.

For Christmas Larch Hill was cleaned and polished as never before. A huge fir tree was put up in the recreation room and Sister Monica supervised the erection of the carved wooden crib in the hallway. Blue had to go to Nurse Griffin to have her leg dressed before the nurse went away for her holiday. Nurse Griffin was rubbing a special oil on to the puckered skin around her knee when Lil ran in.

'Blue, come quick. It's Molly!'

Blue jumped up. She couldn't bear it if anything had happened to the little girl.

'What is it?' she asked, anxious.

'It's good news. It's her da. He's come for her. He's taking her home.'

'Her da!'

'Yeah. He lives in Liverpool. That's where Molly's going. She's packing her things right now while her da talks to Sister Regina.'

Molly going! Blue couldn't believe it. She got to the dormitory in double-quick time, her knee and hands forgotten.

Molly's dark eyes were shining. Blue had never seen her look so happy. 'I told you my daddy would come back for me. I told you!'

Blue swallowed hard. Molly deserved to be with her father, to share a life with him again. She had missed him so much, pined for him, cried for him.

'Here, let me help you, Molly,' she offered, bending down and taking the few washed and worn garments that Molly possessed and folding them up. Lil went and got a thick brown paper bag for the clothes from the cupboard on the landing. She slipped two nightdresses from the home in with the clothes, and some extra vests and knickers too.

'Daddy says we're going to live with my Auntie Maureen and he's got a grand job on the buildings in England.'

Blue tried to smile.

'Isn't it great, Blue! I'll be with my daddy.'

'It's the best news I've heard in a long time, Molly, the very best news.'

Lil watched as Blue brushed and tidied Molly's hair and buttoned up her heavy, red wool coat. She had grown so much it barely fitted her.

'Now listen, Molly, you'll remember at night to wake up and go to the toilet, won't you?'

Molly nodded solemnly. 'I will.'

'Now, give us a hug before you go!'

Molly jumped up on Blue's lap for the very last time. Blue buried her face in the dark curls, hoping to remember Molly's scent forever.

'Molly, hurry on. Your daddy's waiting downstairs for you!' called someone from the landing.

Like a whirlwind, Molly grabbed the bag and ran down the stairs, the rest of them waving and calling goodbye. Blue watched as her father scooped the little girl up in his arms and Molly left Larch Hill children's home forever.

Two days later Santa Claus came to Larch Hill in his big red suit and white beard, laughing and giving out presents to all the boys and girls. Blue got a tennis ball, a set of colouring pencils, a pair of gloves and some sweets. Sitting at the big table on Christmas day, eating turkey and gravy, Blue had thoughts only for her two missing best friends, Molly and Jess.

CHAPTER 21

Cowboys and Indians

The long days of winter passed. January was bitterly cold and wet, and the children could see snow on the Dublin mountains, though none fell in the city. They were forced to stay indoors and play in the recreation room. One Saturday after lunch they were told to line up the wooden benches in rows facing the back wall.

'There must be some kind of meeting,' complained Mary. 'What trouble are we in now?'

The others shrugged and got on with the job. They were well used to following orders without any explanation. In no time at all they had the benches set up. About fifteen minutes later Tommy Lyons, the handyman, set up a small table in the centre of the room and then lifted in a big black box and began to set up some equipment on it. It was the film projector, with its reels of film that flickered on the plain white wall opposite.

They sat on their seats, all hushed in expectation. Sister Agnes stood up. 'Do you know what day today is?'

Confused, everyone shook their heads. 'No, Sister.'

'Saturday,' tried one bright spark.

Sister Agnes managed a smile. 'Yes, well, it is that as well. But today is a very special day, a day of celebration for us all. Today is Saint Brigid's Day, the first of February.

'As it is our saint's feast day,' the nun continued, 'Sister Regina, in her goodness, has decided to provide some entertainment for all you children in her care, and there will be refreshments afterwards for everybody.'

They sat in stunned silence for a few seconds before bursting into spontaneous cheers as the room went dark. The screen flickered into life with the sound and antics of a cartoon mouse.

Blue and Lil and Mary laughed their heads off as the mouse got himself in terrible trouble. There were two more short cartoons and then the main feature, a western about three brothers who wanted to save a town. Blue watched, getting engrossed in the story. It wasn't long before all the cowboys banded together, determined to track down whoever was killing their cattle and burning their homes. The white men blamed the Indians who lived in the open plains close by, and they formed a huge posse to hunt them down.

The Indian village was quiet and peaceful, with women and children going about their business, unaware what was happening. Blue closed her eyes when the cowboys came upon the first Indians. The audience cheered and roared as bows and arrows were pitched against rifles and guns. Blue felt her heart sink and wished that she could warn the Indians about what was going to happen.

Blue held her breath and gasped when the youngest cowboy drew his gun and began to shoot. The audience erupted in cheers as the first Indian fell in the dust. But Blue felt an anger grow inside her. The children went crazy, shouting and whooping when the cowboys tracked down more Indians. Then Blue jumped up and cheered as the first Indian arrow tore through one cowboy's shirt. Within minutes the scene had turned into more than a war on the screen. The rest of the kids cheered for the cowboys and Blue, alone, cheered for the Indians. The noise seemed to get louder and louder.

'Use your arrows!' shouted Blue, as three Indian braves lay hidden in the hills and began to pick off their enemy with their arrows.

'Boo! Boo!' yelled the others, and they stamped their feet in protest.

The screen went suddenly blank and then the lights went up. They all blinked. Sister Regina stood angrily before them.

'The film is over,' she announced. This was greeted by moans of disbelief, as they were all desperate to see the end.

'But what about the end, Sister?' asked Bernie Loftus, a ten-year-old sitting in the front row.

'There will be no end, for you have all disgraced yourselves by your deplorable behaviour.' They could tell by the nun's face there was no budging her. 'It only takes one child to cause an upset, to ruin the enjoyment of others. I will not tolerate this sort of mob behaviour in St Brigid's. Do you hear me?'

'Yes, Sister,' they chorused meekly.

'Especially on our patron saint's feastday,' she continued. 'Disgraceful.'

The curtains were opened, the projector put away, and there was no more mention of refreshments as the children, all angry and disappointed, filed out of the hall.

'Why d'ya have to go starting something and ruining it for us all?' threatened one of the big girls, pushing against Blue as she tried to get out the door.

Blue didn't know what to say and looked around frantically for a bit of support from her own friends. But Lil had disappeared, obviously trying to distance herself from her, and Mary's eyes met hers but she remained silent.

'You should have kept your trap shut!' added a girl called Gina. 'We all wanted to see the film, but you had to go and ruin it for us all.'

Tears stung Blue's eyes as others stuck out their tongues or called her names as they walked by.

Blue wanted to say they were the ones who had started it with their cheering and foot-banging, but she knew from the angry glances around her that it was useless. Sister Regina stopped her in the corridor and lectured her aloud about how one rotten apple in a barrel can spoil all the rest of the crop. Embarrassed and humiliated, she went to bed not bothering to go down for tea, and wishing she had never seen the stupid film. It wasn't fair that she was the one being blamed by everyone.

She was surprised to see Sister Monica appear in the dormitory, and pretended to be asleep in the hope that the old nun would leave her alone. She couldn't face any more telling-off.

'That was brave today, child,' said the old nun. 'Standing up for your beliefs. Prepared to speak out against injustice!'

Blue didn't fully understand what the nun was talking about, but she opened her eyes and turned around in the bed.

'Ah, good. I'm glad to see you're awake. Today you stood up for your beliefs, something few are brave enough to do.'

Blue was puzzled. All she'd done was cheer for the Indians instead of the cowboys.

'It is always hard to stand up and fight for your fellow man, to speak out against things that are wrong,' explained Sister Monica, her monkey-face sincere. 'You are an unusual child, Bernadette!'

Blue could hardly believe what she was hearing. The nun was *agreeing* with her! 'There was a time when I too stood up for my beliefs, and I too was punished. Africa, that was my punishment in their eyes! I was sent on the missions to a place where I did God's work, and served him with all my heart. The place where I learned to fight like a lion for people who needed my help. Now I am back in Ireland, old and broken from perhaps too many days in the hot sun, but you know, Blue, I wouldn't change a single day of it and if I had to do it again I would happily stand shoulder to shoulder with my African brothers and sisters in their struggles.'

Blue looked at the old nun, with her leathery skin and tired eyes and stooped figure, and wanted to wrap her arms around her.

'You and I are more alike than you imagine,' said the nun, smiling. She stretched her tiny wrinkled hand into her habit and drew out two iced buns wrapped in a white hankie. 'You haven't eaten, so I thought you might like these. Sister Patricia made them for the community, but at my age too many sweet things aren't good for you. You have them!'

Blue sat up, hunger getting the better of her as she took the sweet cakes and gobbled them quickly. Sister Monica brushed the crumbs off the bed.

'Thank you,' Blue mumbled.

They could hear the sound of footsteps outside in the corridor and on the stairs as the others came to get ready for bed. Sister Monica turned away, excusing herself as Lil and Mary and the rest of the girls appeared.

Nobody said anything to her and Blue pulled the blanket back around her. She could hear them whispering and making comments. They were all still grumbling and giving out about missing the end of the film.

'Blue O'Malley is a rotten spoilsport.' Blue recognised the hard voice of Joan. 'She doesn't care that she spoiled all our fun! We should do something about her.'

From the corner of her eye Blue could see the round face of her enemy, with her pudding-bowl hair and buck teeth, and, unable to stop herself, she leapt out of bed and found herself standing in front of the other girl in her nightclothes.

'You take back what you said about me!' she demanded. 'I'm not a spoilsport!'

'Will not.'

'You will.'

The other girl shook her head obstinately.

In a sudden burst of fury, Blue butted into her and knocked her on to an adjacent bed. Then Joan pulled Blue down on top of her and the two of them dragged and punched at each other, the rest of the girls, excited, screaming encouragement.

Blue could feel her anger and temper rise. She wanted to squash her enemy's face, push her into the pillows, suffocate her, get her to shut up. She was strong, even though she was younger than Joan and smaller.

'Get her off me!' groaned Joan.

'Say you're sorry!' Blue insisted. She could feel the other girl weaken, about to give in.

'What in the name of heaven is going on in here?' Too late Blue spotted the flick of the black habit, as Sister Agnes pulled her off the other girl. 'Bernadette O'Malley! I can't say I'm surprised. You have been spoiling for a fight all day.'

Blue stood up straight and pushed her hair from her face. She was out of breath, panting with exertion and excitement. Joan got up slowly too.

'Fighting like two cats, I won't stand for it!'

'She started it, Sister!' wailed Joan. 'Ask the others, they'll tell you the truth.'

A few heads nodded. No one spoke.

Sister Agnes believed her. She stared at Blue disdainfully. 'I think it's about time you learned to cool your heels, young lady. The rest of you get back into bed and I want strict silence, do you hear me?'

Blue watched them crawl silently into their beds while she stood there in her nightdress. Lil cast her a pitying look.

'Follow me!' ordered the nun.

Blue walked behind her out into the dark corridor and then upstairs to the landing where a statue of their patron saint stood.

'I think you need to make atonement, contemplate your bad behaviour,' said the nun. 'I always find Saint Brigid a good saint to pray to if in need of guidance. You will kneel here on the landing for the next few hours praying and asking for forgiveness.'

'I can't, Sister.'

The nun looked taken aback.

'I can't kneel, Sister.'

'Then you can stand,' the nun ordered.

Blue blinked. It was cold and dark on the landing and she didn't want to stand here all on her own. She thought of crying and begging for forgiveness, to be let go back to the dormitory, but seeing the steely, cold look on the nun's face she knew that the cruel woman in front of her would not change her mind.

'You will stand here for the rest of the night and pray,' Sister Agnes warned, 'and I will come for you in the morning when I rise to say my early prayers.'

Blue swallowed hard. It wasn't fair. But she would accept her punishment; she had no choice. She watched as Sister Agnes went up the corridor and turned in the door to the rooms where the nuns slept.

She shivered in her nightdress, her bare feet cold. She stamped up and down gently, trying to warm them and keep her circulation going. She stared at the plaster statue, taking in the kind face and gentle eyes of the saint who was known to be loving and caring. She tried to pray, going through the litany of prayers they had been taught, saying them aloud. She repeated them one after another in a constant rhyme of words and sounds for what seemed like hours. Her own voice was the only sound she heard.

The whole house was still.

She was freezing and swung her arms back and forth in the vain hope of keeping warm, marching silently over and back, over and back. She was tired and cold and hungry and would give anything to be back in her bed in the dormitory with the others instead of out on the landing all on her own. She yawned, trying to stay awake.

'Blue!'

She turned around to see Lil creeping up the stairs.

'I brought you this,' whispered her friend. It was the woollen underblanket from her bed. 'You'll get your death standing here all night in the cold. Wrap this around you at least.'

Tears filled her eyes – poor Lil would be in big trouble if she was caught helping her.

'Lil, thanks a lot. You'd better get back to bed.'

She watched her friend slip back downstairs as she wrapped herself in the rough blanket. At least she was a bit warmer now. She stared at the saint with the kind face and gentle eyes.

'You took my friend Jess away,' she confided, 'and now with Molly gone too, I've nothing to stay for. I've got to get out of here! I'm going to run away.'

CHAPTER 22

The Plan

She kept it a secret for a long time, not trusting anyone to know that she was going to run away. She hated Sister Regina and Sister Agnes and she was fed up with life in the orphanage. The idea of escape grew and grew in her mind.

She was not sure where she would go to but she had some money hidden away – a half crown from the Hickeys as well as Jess's one pound, twelve shillings and sixpence. Surely that was enough to buy a ticket to get far away from the nuns and Larch Hill? She wondered would she have enough to get to Liverpool? Liverpool was where Molly was. Liverpool was where The Beatles lived – John, Paul, George and Ringo. Lil said they were the best band in the world. Her mind was addled with plotting and planning, trying to work out how she could get away and not get caught.

'Blue, are you listening to me?' asked Mary one evening while Blue was thinking about her plan.

'What?'

'You're not listening, I knew it!'

'Go on, I'm sorry.' Blue could hear the worry in Mary's voice.

'I was trying to tell you about Tommy. His teacher said to him yesterday about working hard in his new school.'

'New school?'

'Yes! Why would the teacher mention a new school unless he's going to leave Larch Hill?' Mary was almost hysterical, her eyes wild and scared-looking. 'I don't want him to go, Blue. I can't bear it.'

Blue's heart sank. She didn't know how Mary would get over losing her little brother. He was her only family.

'They can't send Tommy away. It's not fair.'

'You know the boys only stay here till they're eight, and then they go to the boys' home. You know that, Mary.'

'He's not going. They can't send Tommy there. I'm going to go and talk to Sister Regina about it.'

Blue couldn't believe it, Mary going to the head nun's office.

'Will you come with me?'

Blue swallowed hard. Sister Regina hated her.

'I don't mean you have to come in, Blue, but just walk up to the door with me so I don't get cold feet and run away.'

''Course I will.'

Mary's face was strained and pale the next day when she stood outside the head nun's door, trying to get the courage to knock. Blue was nervous for her.

'Go on, Mary,' she urged.

'I'm doing this for Tommy,' Mary said firmly, clenching her hand into a fist and knocking loudly on the heavy door.

'Come in,' said the voice.

Blue squeezed her hand before she disappeared inside.

She waited down the corridor. Mary reappeared a few minutes later, and walked right past her.

'Mary! Mary, how did it go?'

Mary Doyle, eyes red-rimmed, didn't say a solitary word.

Ten days later Tommy was gone. He and two other small boys, Davey Lynch and Paul Byrne, no longer sat at the table in the corner of the dining hall or chased around the corridors after each other. The three of them had been moved to a home for older boys.

'I didn't even get a chance to say a proper goodbye to him,' Mary repeated over and over again. She sat at the table in despair. In school she paid no attention to the teacher and did no homework. In the yard she refused to play, and at night she pulled the blankets over her head and gave in to her tears in the dark.

'God, it's awful,' declared Lil. 'Do you think she's going mad?'

Blue had to admit she was really worried. Her plans for running away were pushed to the back of her mind as she couldn't contemplate leaving Mary at a time like this.

'Girls, be kind to Mary Doyle for the moment,' urged Sister Carmel, who was shocked by the change in the girl and concerned for her well-being.

Three weeks later a letter came. Mary tore the envelope open. It was from Tommy.

> Dear Mary,
> I love you.
> I miss you.
> I am happy.
> Tommy xxx

Mary read and re-read the letter again and again, as if it contained some coded message or hidden meaning. There was no address, just the simple, lined white paper. She studied the envelope.

'Look, Blue. It says Galway. That's where they must have sent him.'

Blue was relieved. She hoped that in some way Mary could get back to her old self, now that she knew her little brother was safe and well.

Once again she began to hatch her own plans, dreaming of being free of the grey walls and strict routines of Larch Hill. Timing was the important thing, as she would have to make sure no one was watching her, and she lay awake at night trying to plot the best way of getting out of Larch Hill.

'Blue, are you awake?' whispered Mary.

She nodded.

'Can you keep a secret?'

''Course I can. Cross my heart!' She sat up. Mary had been acting so strange lately.

'I'm getting out of here.'

'Getting out! But how?'

'I don't know yet,' confided Mary, 'but I'm going to Galway to find Tommy. They can't separate us. I won't let them.'

Blue took a deep breath. She'd been half expecting this. Mary wasn't the type to forget about her brother. She would go to the ends of the earth for the people she loved.

'Will you help me?'

Blue didn't know what to say. She had been planning her own escape, but looking at the excited, freckled face she realised that she would have to bring Mary Doyle with her.

CHAPTER 23

Searching for Tommy

Two are better than one, that's what they told themselves as they plotted their escape. The best time to make their getaway was early in the morning, after breakfast, when the children from Larch Hill marched across the yard and down a short laneway to join all the other children from the streets nearby going to the local primary school. In those few minutes they were in a no-man's land between the orphanage and the school, with no one directly in charge of them.

'That's the very best time for us to go,' insisted Blue. 'The nuns will think we're at school and Mrs Brady will probably think I'm with the nurse again and you can let on the day before that you're sick.'

Mary agreed. It was a good plan. She didn't have any money, so they would just have to make do with what Blue had saved.

They waited for the opportunity and then, one bright March day, they fell back from the others in the yard, and scrambled behind the low walls where the bins were. Minutes later, when the bell had sounded and class had started, they dashed across the yard, climbed up over the back wall, then jumped down to the freedom of an overgrown and rubbish-strewn back alley, where a startled rat darted in front of them. The two girls took to their heels.

They were out of breath and panting by the time they reached the bus stop. Mary blazed red as a woman with a shopping basket stared curiously at them. Blue gave her a dig in the ribs, hoping she wouldn't give the game away by mentioning the orphanage if the woman questioned her. The minute the bus appeared, they made their way upstairs, away from the woman and her shopping basket.

'Mary, will you stop looking so guilty!' Blue whispered.

'Janey, my heart's beating so fast I thought that woman would hear it!'

'Will you shut up now and stop drawing attention to us.'

They stared out the window as the bus headed towards the city centre, filling up with passengers at every stop. The conductor came and took their fares. At last the bus come to a juddering halt and the passengers tumbled out.

'There's the river Liffey,' Mary pointed out excitedly as Blue stopped a man in a business suit and asked him the way to the train station. Anxious to get out of Dublin, they ran along the busy city quays, following his directions. Kingsbridge railway station was crowded with people, and the two girls joined the long queue to buy tickets.

'Two to Galway,' said Blue firmly when their turn came at last.

'Return?' asked the man behind the glass panel.

'Return?' Blue hesitated, unsure.

'Are ye coming back to Dublin later this month or on the same day? It makes a difference.'

'We're staying in Galway with our Granny, and we won't be coming back.'

'Then it's two singles you want. That'll be one pound twelve shillings and sixpence.'

'How much?' gasped Mary. It was nearly all the money they had.

'You heard me!' said the man, getting irritated now as the crowd became agitated behind them. 'Do you want the tickets or not?'

'What time does the train leave?' asked Blue.

'Well, you missed the earlier one. The next one will be leaving around six o'clock and will get you into Galway by half-past nine.'

'I'm sorry, but we'll have to come back later,' apologised Blue, grabbing hold of Mary's jacket and pulling her out of the line, ignoring the annoyed stares of the other waiting passengers.

Mary looked like she was about to burst into tears. Blue didn't want to attract attention so she dragged her friend into the ladies' toilet.

'What are we going to do?' Mary wailed. 'We'll have no money left over, and the next train isn't till tonight! How are we ever going to find Tommy?'

Blue had to admit she hadn't reckoned on the price of the tickets being so high and the fact that there wasn't another train for hours, but she wasn't going to give up now.

'We'll never get to Galway,' sobbed Mary, 'and I'll never see Tommy again.'

'Shush, shush,' Blue soothed, trying to calm her friend down.

'Miss the train to Galway, loveys?' asked the toilet attendant, who was busy polishing the mirrors. 'People are always missing trains, but you could always get the bus. It takes a bit longer, but sure, it's only half the price.'

'Half the price?'

The cleaning lady explained to them where to get the bus and wished them luck.

The two of them ran helter-skelter back the way they had come. They arrived at Busaras only to find that they'd missed the morning bus to Galway too, but that there was another one in the afternoon.

'That'll do us fine,' grinned Mary.

'What'll we do while we're waiting?" asked Blue, not willing to sit in the bus station for hours.

'I suppose we could walk around the shops for a while, once nobody notices us.'

They both agreed and headed back towards Nelson's Pillar in the middle of O'Connell Street. The city centre was busy with shoppers and workers. Cars and buses all crowded into Dublin's main street. A Garda with white gloves directed the traffic in the distance and they both automatically turned away from him.

'There's the GPO where they fought in the Easter Rising.' Blue tried to imagine the street in 1916 with the buildings in flames and the street overrun with soldiers and filled with the sound of gunfire.

'There's Clery's!' gasped Mary, leading the way to the huge department store. 'Let's go in here.' She pushed in the heavy glass door with the polished brass handles.

A shop assistant watched them and Blue could feel her eyes follow them as they walked by the wooden counters with their displays of handbags and scarves. A customer finally called her away to wrap a scarf she had been trying on.

Spotting a sign for the toy department they headed downstairs. They walked through rows of pots and pans and bowls and glasses and trays of silver cutlery first, all proclaiming to be the perfect wedding present.

'Look!' shouted Mary at last.

The two of them stood in awe, taking in the paradise of the children's toy department. There was a whole row of dolls, from a huge one the size of a child to lots of tiny ones, with every possible colour of hair and eyes. Each had an outfit – a check coat and matching scarf, a pink party dress, a riding outfit, a bride's outfit. There were baby dolls that sucked on bottles and could wee, there were dolls with long hair to comb or plait, dolls that cried if you tilted them forward. Dolls that were soft and cuddly and dolls that had hard, plastic faces and bodies. Neither of them had ever seen the like of it. The place was almost empty and they played a delicious game of pretend, in which they could each pick their favourite doll. They could have stayed there for the day, imagining they were allowed to play with all the toys, but they spotted the security officer ambling over towards them.

'He's watching us,' whispered Blue. 'Let's get a move on.'

Reluctantly they left Clery's, suddenly realising how hungry and thirsty they were and wishing they'd brought something to eat. The cafés and restaurants were full, and their stomachs groaned as the smell of food assailed them.

'Janey, I'm starving!' said Mary. 'Do you think we've enough money to buy some food?'

They looked around and spotted a small kiosk that sold doughnuts and they bought one each, plus a small bottle of lemonade, asking the man for two straws. They gulped down the doughy rings and took small sips of the fizzy drink, saving the rest for later.

Across the road they spotted a large bookshop and Blue persuaded Mary to go inside with her. She had never seen so many books in her life, and longed to read every one of them.

''Tis only stupid books,' sighed Mary, who still stumbled over letters and words and had no interest in reading. Blue managed to distract her for a while by pointing her towards the stationery section with its coloured pens and pencils and crayon sets, while she scanned the vast bookshelves.

Back outside, they turned a corner and found themselves in Moore Street. Voices called to them all along the street.

'Bunches of green grapes – bring them to the hospital – treat yourselves – all the way from Italy.'

Fruit and vegetables were piled up on every stall, the women gossiping to each other as they shouted out their wares. Mary and Blue watched as they weighed out potatoes and carrots and plums and onions, and, if the customer was nice, adding an extra one for luck, before tipping the stuff into a paper bag which they twirled in the air as they fastened it.

Finally it was time to catch the bus for Galway. They got their tickets, then fell into their seats, anxious and excited at the thought of the journey. The driver revved the engine for ages before he finally closed the doors and set off.

'Don't tell anyone what we're doing!' cautioned Blue. 'Pretend we're sisters and are going to visit our Granny.'

Mary nodded nervously. Both of them were only too aware that they looked nothing like sisters. But the bus was half-empty

The bus pushed its way through the city streets up along the quays, then out past rows of red-brick houses and terraces, until it finally left the city behind. Soon they were in the country, passing through one small town after another.

'Do you think they'll have missed us yet?' Mary whispered nervously.

Blue shrugged. They had timed it well. The staff in Larch Hill wouldn't realise till at least midday or, if they were lucky, three o'clock that they had not been at school and the teachers would simply have marked them absent. Mary had pretended to the others that morning that she wasn't feeling well and told them she was going to the infirmary.

But by now the nuns would definitely know they were missing and would have a search party out looking for them. They were both tired and anxious and the lulling movement of the bus made them drowsy, but they didn't dare fall asleep or let their guard down. It was almost half-past six when they finally reached Galway city, the two of them yawning and stretching as they tried to rouse themselves.

'We're here, we're here!' shouted Mary.

'Eyre Square,' called the driver. 'You two girls okay?' he asked as they clambered down off the bus. 'Is there someone to meet you?'

Blue spotted an old woman with white hair and a green cardigan, with a little terrier on a lead, approaching the bus stop on the square.

'Oh Mary, there's Granny and she's brought Patch to meet us.' She waved wildly and pushed her friend in the right direction.

A look of confusion crossed the woman's face as she searched the crowd, trying to see past the girl with the flailing arms. Satisfied, the driver bent down to help someone with their luggage.

They stood in the corner of Eyre Square, totally unsure of what to do or where to begin the search for Tommy. Blue stopped an old man and a young woman, probably his daughter, to ask, 'Do you know where Saint Gerard's orphanage is?'

The daughter looked unsure, but the old man was in no doubt. ''Tis about four miles out the Salthill road, towards Spiddal.'

'Four miles!' They couldn't walk four miles, not at this time of the evening. 'Can you get a bus there?'

'Aye, there's a bus, but you won't get one now till tomorrow.'

Mary looked like she was about to break down and cry. Blue stood beside her, unsure what to do.

'We're going out that way, Daddy,' said the young woman. 'We could drop them a good part of the way. Is that any use?' she asked, looking at Blue.

Any use? It was perfect and, not believing their good fortune, the girls found themselves sitting in the back seat of a Morris Minor, surrounded by packages. The daughter was driving and if she was curious as to their destination she didn't let on.

'Do you have someone in Saint Gerard's?' asked the old man.

'My brother,' Mary blurted out.

'It's his birthday today,' interrupted Blue, 'and we were supposed to bring him a present from our Mammy 'cause she's not too well, but we got delayed and didn't realise the time.'

'Well, you can't let him down, then,' smiled the driver. 'Listen, I'll drop you here, right near the place. It's only about a five-minute walk.

Take a right turn over there and you can't miss it.'

They said a huge thank you, and when the car was gone took to their heels and ran the rest of the way.

A large statue of a saint, whom they presumed was Saint Gerard, guarded the gates to a tall, white-washed building that was the boys' home. The gate was unlocked and in the distance in a small field a crowd of older boys were kicking a football around in the dusk.

'They're the big boys. Tommy won't be with them.' Mary's face was so white that Blue wondered would she be sick. 'He must be inside.'

She could feel her own stomach doing cartwheels, turning over at the thought of being caught. Over and over again they had discussed coming to the orphanage and seeing Tommy, but nothing beyond that. They'd forgotten the most important part of the plan: what would they do with Tommy once they found him?

'Come on,' hissed Mary, leading the way around the back. They could hear shouting and voices coming from upstairs. 'They must be getting ready for bed. Tommy'll be there with them.'

They went through a door and crept up the dark wooden stairs, praying that a brother or one of the boys wouldn't come along. Up to one landing, then another, they found themselves amongst a line of small boys pushing and shoving outside a bathroom. They searched the faces trying to see if young Tommy was there.

'Girls!' shouted a young fellow, sounding the alarm. 'Girls!' he shouted again, even louder.

'Shut up, Conor, or I'll thump you,' ordered Blue, immediately recognising him from Larch Hill. 'Mary and I are trying to find her brother, Tommy Doyle. He's a new boy, only here about two weeks.'

'I know him, miss,' offered a small, scrawny boy with a face like a mouse and two sticking-out ears. 'Tommy sleeps in my room, that one just down there. He's always sniffling and crying and the brothers don't like him 'cos he causes a fuss.'

Sniffling and crying! Mary didn't like the sound of that and looked like she was ready to murder anyone who touched her little brother. The boy pointed towards a dormitory along the corridor.

'This way!' Mary announced in her big-sister voice, and she led the way to the small dormitory in the middle of the corridor. They pushed open the door, and they both instantly recognised the small figure with the tousled hair, trying to fasten up a pair of striped pyjamas much too big for him.

'Tommy!'

Brother and sister flew into each other's arms and held on like they would never let go again. Mary's face was like a ghost as she hugged and kissed little Tommy. Then she sat on the bed beside him.

'I told you I'd find you, didn't I?'

The small pale face with the freckles and blue eyes nodded. 'I knew you'd come,' was all he said as he buried his face again in her jacket and school cardigan.

Blue swallowed hard, not wanting to cry, but suddenly envious of Mary and her brother.

A whisper went around the corridor and the rest of the boys stayed outside leaving the two of them alone. Suddenly Conor ran in.

'It's Brother Benildus, he's on his way up the stairs,' he warned. 'We can delay him for a few minutes but he checks all the rooms every night before we go to bed, honest.'

'Mary, come on!' urged Blue. 'We've got to get out of here before we're discovered.'

Her friend sat obstinately on the bed, clutching her little brother.

'I'm not leaving him, Blue, do you hear! I don't care what the brothers say or do. He's my brother and I promised Mammy I'd look after him. They can't just go and split us up. I won't let them!' Tommy had a firm grip on his sister and refused to let go of her.

Blue was almost out of her mind with panic as she heard the heavy steps on the corridor and the adult voice asking the boys had they washed their hands and faces.

'Mary, come on!' she pleaded. 'We have to get out of here or we'll be caught. You've seen Tommy now, but we've got to get going or else we'll be in right trouble.'

Mary turned her back, ignoring her. 'I'm not leaving him.'

Blue didn't know what to do.

'Over here!' shouted Conor, pulling Blue's hand, 'to the window.' It was almost dark outside, but Blue could see the metal railings and bars of the fire escape.

'You have to be careful as the bottom part is wired off to stop people climbing it ...'

He didn't have to say any more, it was an escape route and that was all that mattered.

'Mary,' she begged one last time, but seeing the tears and the desperate look on young Tommy's stricken face she knew Mary would not leave her brother. Conor held the window open as far as it would go. It was no more than a strip but she was skinny enough to squeeze through. Conor closed the window firmly and pulled the curtains closed after her. She didn't stay to listen to what Brother

Benildus would say when he discovered Mary. She began to move silently down the steps, praying she wouldn't slip or lose her footing. She didn't dare think what the consequences for Mary and Tommy would be or what the brothers in Saint Gerard's would do to her friend. She had to concentrate on herself now and on getting away. At the bottom of the metal stairs, where it was wired off, she made a wild jump on to the grass, wincing with pain as she hit the ground. Her right ankle landed on a stone. But she could walk. What would she do now?

She couldn't stay here. The brothers might search the grounds for her if Mary or the boys told them she had come with a friend. She had to get away as quickly as possible. She limped down the driveway and back out the main gates on to the narrow road. It was four miles to Galway and she had no option but to walk.

The night was dry at least, and it wasn't cold. She tried not to think of the pain, and pretended she was a scout out hunting for food in the darkness of the African savannah, letting the moon be her guide.

CHAPTER 24

Rain Rain

Galway was deserted in the early morning and Blue curled up on a park bench in Eyre Square to rest, her mind in turmoil. She couldn't stay here. The brothers from Saint Gerard's might be looking for her. The city was too small, they could easily track her down. She'd have to go back to Dublin where she could disappear among the crowds. She'd kept her promise to Mary to help find her brother, but now she had to think of herself.

The sound of vans and lorries woke her as Galway began to stir. Porters with tall brushes came out to sweep the steps of the Great Southern hotel. Soon the shutters would go up in the shops, and the banks and offices would open for the day's business and trading. She watched as people arrived for the early-morning train, carrying their cases and bags towards the train station around the corner. If only she had a ticket for the train to Dublin. Curious, she followed a group of women who got out of a big black car.

'Hurry on, Anna, hurry on!' called one of them.

'I'm coming, Aunt Teresa,' said a younger one, 'but I've got to get my ticket.'

'No time for that, dear, or we'll miss getting seats together. Hurry up and we'll pay on the train.'

Pay on the train! Blue couldn't believe her ears. So you could pay on the train. Imagine! The group of women dragged several huge cases, a couple of hat boxes and a zip-up hold-all down to the station entrance. Blue followed them along the platform as they tried to manoeuvre the bags up on to the train.

'Give us a hand, Anna,' called the aunt, struggling with the heaviest bag.

Blue stepped forward. 'Here, let me help you with that,' she offered, humping the big suitcase with all her strength as she stepped on to the train.

'Oh, thank you, dear,' smiled the woman.

Blue filed into the same carriage as the women and squeezed into the seat next to the door, saying nothing as the rest of the carriage filled up. She waited, heart thumping, as the doors were shut and the train began to shunt out of the station. Blue turned her face to the wall. They couldn't throw her off the train, could they? They'd at least take her to the next stop and put her off there.

As the train got going the carriage filled with the laughter and chatter of the group of women around her. They were on their way to a wedding in Dublin. Blue kept an eye on the door, ready to run when she spotted the conductor coming to check the tickets. A boy came by with a trolley of tea and coffee and sandwiches. She felt in her pocket. She hadn't enough even for a sandwich. The woman beside her ordered tea and ham sandwiches and some biscuits. Blue gulped hard and her stomach flipped over with hunger watching the woman eat, her eyes almost popping out of her head when she saw the discarded piece of buttered crust and a digestive biscuit. The woman excused herself to go to the toilet, and in a flash, when no one was looking, Blue had wolfed down the left-overs.

She felt warm, and the motion of the train made her drowsy. Her head got heavier and heavier and she longed to sleep. Then she heard the words: 'Tickets, please. Tickets, please.'

The conductor was coming down the train. She had to get away. She jumped up and made for the toilet. Closing the door after her and slipping the lock across, she sat down in the tiny space to hide. Would the woman tell the conductor about her? Would the conductor come looking for her?

She waited and waited in the tiny space, the noise of the engine getting louder, the train moving faster as they flew through the countryside. She was able to wash her hands and face and sit on the toilet seat all at the same time. Her ankle ached and she dampened some toilet paper to wrap it up. After what seemed like half an hour she wondered should she come out. She opened the door a crack, peeped out and saw two people waiting to use the facilities. Checking that the conductor was gone from the carriage, she went back to her seat. The woman had fallen asleep, and was snoring slightly, her mouth open. Blue slipped in beside her. Relief washed over her as she settled down for the rest of the journey.

Rain spattered against the windows as they approached Dublin city and green fields turned to grey city streets and roofs. The woman beside Blue began to refresh her make-up, then she stood up and put on her heavy raincoat. The train got slower and slower, eventually coming to a grinding halt. All the passengers stood up to leave, gathering their belongings. Blue was determined to stay with the wedding group as they departed the train and station. She kept her head down and passed quickly through the gates before anyone could notice her. She walked along under the high station ceilings, across the tiled entrance hall and out onto the street. It was raining heavily. Some of the travellers joined the queue for taxis, others had friends to meet them, but Blue was all alone.

She stepped out into the pelting rain and began to walk towards the city centre. Her hair hung in rats' tails and her jacket and skirt were soaked. She could feel the water leaking in through holes in her shoes. She just had to keep walking – she wasn't sure where to, but she felt that if she stayed on her feet and kept moving she'd be all right. She tried to ignore the pain in her foot as she walked along by the river wall. The heavy rain soaked her face as the wind swept upriver. It was a busy quay. Cars hooted and heavy trucks exiting Guinness's brewery splashed her as they thundered by. Blue cursed them under her breath.

Then a car slowed down beside her, but she ignored it. The driver beeped and honked his horn again and again until she finally looked up. It was a taxi-cab. She hadn't the money for a fare, so she ignored him.

But he honked his horn at her again, and rolled down his window.

'Get in!' he shouted.

She stopped, ready to shout at him and tell him to leave her alone when she recognised him. It was Jimmy Mooney, the taxi driver who had taken them all to the zoo and who had brought her home from hospital.

'Get in, girl, you're soaked to the skin.'

She hesitated as he opened the door for her.

'I'm all wet,' she warned. 'I'll ruin your car.'

'That don't matter. Get in!'

She clambered into the back of the cab, a pool of water forming immediately on the floor of the car.

'What in heaven's name are you doing out on a day like this?' he demanded, pulling back out into the traffic. 'Have the nuns gone mad?'

She stayed silent. She caught a glimpse of him staring at her in the mirror.

'I spotted you coming out of the station,' he said. 'What were you doing there?'

'I was in Galway.'

'Galway?'

'With a friend.'

'A friend?' he harrumphed. 'I'll take you back to Larch Hill.'

'No!' she shouted, trying to open the door of the car, 'I'm not going back there.'

'Not going back?'

The traffic was heavy and the car had almost come to a standstill, enabling him to turn around to face her.

'I don't live there any more.'

A silence hung between them.

'Well, then, where do you live? Give me the address and I'll take you home.'

She felt wet and cold and shivery and although she wanted to be smart and lie and make up an address, she couldn't. She sniffed. Jimmy Mooney was looking at her.

'What's the matter, kid?'

'I've run away.'

'Run away! Holy God, you've run away from Sister Agnes and Sister Regina and the rest of them?'

She nodded dumbly, realising the enormity of what she'd done.

'I can't go back. I won't go back.'

The traffic lights had turned green and Jimmy began to drive. Blue realised eventually that he was driving around in a circle, passing the same shops and offices again.

'Don't send me back there!' she pleaded. 'Please, Jimmy, don't.'

He kept driving, obviously trying to decide the right thing to do. 'Sister Regina will be fuming, I'll give you that, and you'll be in right old trouble, but you have to go back.'

'I'll get thrashed. She'll use the leather ...'

She could see the concern in his eyes, the indecision.

'The nuns wouldn't do that.'

'She would, that's what happened before ...' she trailed off. 'I hate Larch Hill. I hate them all. Stop! Let me out of the car!'

She tried to pull open the handle of door. 'I'm not going back there!'

Jimmy Mooney tried to concentrate on driving in the downpour. The insides of his windows were fogged up and his windscreen wipers couldn't keep pace with the lashing rain. Plus, he was trying to stop the child jumping out of a moving vehicle. She looked wild and crazy. Eventually he made up his mind and headed off purposefully in a different direction.

'Where are you taking me?' Blue wailed.

'I'm taking you home.'

'I don't want to go back to Larch Hill. I don't want to go there.'

'No. Home to my place,' he explained. 'Ma is there. She'll know what to do.'

She sank back in the seat with relief as Jimmy checked to make sure she wasn't going to try and escape again.

'Ma will have to know what to do,' he said firmly.

CHAPTER 25

Iveagh Terrace

Jimmy showed Blue into the small kitchen at Iveagh Terrace where Nance Mooney was sitting by the fire with her feet up on a leatherette pouffe.

'Where in heaven's name did you find the child, Jimmy?' she asked, jumping up to get a towel so that Blue could dry herself.

'The girl is half-drowned with the rain and half-starved too by the look of it. Her name's Bernadette O'Malley, but they call her "Blue",' he reminded her. 'You remember her, don't you? From the day at the zoo? She's one of the kids from Larch Hill. I spotted her down by the station.'

'Larch Hill?' Nance Mooney bent closer to get a good look at her. 'Yes, I remember her.'

Blue suddenly felt cold and shivery and weak, too tired even to think.

'Poor pet, she looks all done in,' murmured the elderly woman, her double chin wobbling with concern. 'Jimmy, go get a blanket and the red dressing-gown from my room. We'd better get her out of these wet clothes before she catches her death of cold.'

Ten minutes later Blue found herself wrapped in a huge, soft, wool dressing gown, a check blanket spread over her lap and knees, and her hair combed out on her shoulders to dry. She watched Mrs Mooney make her a mug of hot, milky tea and set sausages and rashers on the pan to fry.

'What were the nuns doing letting her out on a day like this?' she tut-tutted as she pricked the sizzling sausages.

'She ran away, Ma.' Jimmy glanced over at the girl. 'The nuns had nothing to do with it.'

'Ran away? She's a runaway!' Mrs Mooney looked at Blue, her expression curious and concerned. 'Is that true, child?'

Blue nodded, miserable. All her defiance and energy was deflated like a big balloon from which all the air had escaped.

'Well, I never! What are we going to do? We'd better send her straight back to the nuns. By now they probably have the Guards and half the country out looking for her.'

'I don't want to go back,' Blue burst out. 'I hate it there. Please don't make me go back to Larch Hill, Mrs Mooney, please!'

Blue's eyes filled with tears and she had a choking feeling in the back of her throat. She looked at the big man with his blinking brown eyes and balding head, and the small, plump woman, with her neatly permed grey hair, staring at her. These people were her only hope. But what could they do for her? She would soon be back with the nuns, for sure. Her heart sank.

Jimmy put two spoonfuls of sugar in his tea, and stirred it slowly, considering the situation.

'Have you family, friends, anyone you can go to?' asked Mrs Mooney.

Blue shook her head. 'No one. I'm on my own.'

A stricken look passed over Nance Mooney's face as she realised the implication of not having a relation in the world to call on or cling to. 'My God, you poor little thing.' Instinctively, she reached forward and hugged the girl. Blue sank into the warm flesh and scent of soap and rosewater. Her head snuggled into the plump shoulders and breast.

'Here, Ma, the sausages are burning,' said Jimmy.

Minutes later they were all sitting around the table. Hunger overwhelmed Blue and she devoured her plate of sausages and rashers, along with three slices of fried bread and another mug of tea.

'There isn't a pick on the child! She needs feeding up, if you ask me,' announced Mrs Mooney. 'Don't they feed you proper in that place?'

Blue thought of the plates of disgusting, dreary food that was served in the home – lumpy porridge, stale bread, soapy potatoes, squelchy mash and runny, watery eggs, and, if there was meat, it was either too fatty or too greasy or too gristly to enjoy. The serving size never changed and there was never enough for the children to eat.

'They do feed us,' she hesitated, 'but it's nothing like this.'

A pleased look spread across the woman's face.

'Well, what are we going to do with her?' insisted Jimmy.

Blue looked from one face to the other, hoping they wouldn't send her back.

'She looks exhausted,' said his mother. 'Maybe she could stay a while here and rest, get her breath back and have a bit of a sleep.'

'I have to go back to work, Ma. She'd have to stay here with you.'

'Away you go then, Jimmy,' the woman said. 'We'll have a think about it and decide what to do when you get back. Don't worry, I'll take care of her.'

Blue watched through sleepy eyes as Jimmy pulled on his heavy jacket and got his car keys. She wondered would he arrive back with the police in tow to arrest her or with Sister Regina to drag her back to Larch Hill.

Mrs Mooney fussed around the kitchen tidying up, her feet encased in two big pink furry slippers, her ankles and legs wrapped in flesh-coloured tights that emphasised her varicose veins.

Blue felt warm and drowsy and full.

It was almost dark when she woke to find Mrs Mooney looking at her.

'I'm sorry,' she yawned. 'Did I fall asleep?'

'You've been dead to the world for the past four hours. I didn't want to disturb you in case I gave you a fright.'

'Is Jimmy back?'

'Not yet. He'll be home in a while.'

Blue sighed to herself. No doubt he'd be back any minute to drive her to Larch Hill.

'I've got the dinner on, a nice shepherd's pie. Do you like shepherd's pie?'

Blue shrugged. She had no idea what it was. 'I'm not used to fancy food,' she explained.

Mrs Mooney burst out laughing. She laughed so hard she had to sit back down in her wide armchair.

'Well, I never! That's a good one. Shepherd's pie a fancy food! You are a funny little thing. Do you know how to play cards?'

Blue shook her head. Sometimes a deck of cards would appear at the children's home but usually there were cards missing from it. She could play Snap and Fish in the Pool, but these games usually caused rows and the cards ended up being flung in the air with annoyance.

'Then it's high time you learned.' Nance Mooney took out a pack of cards from the drawer and dealt them each a hand, explaining the symbols and numbers to Blue and their worth. 'We'll play Twenty-one.'

Engrossed, Blue followed the instructions carefully, examining her cards and working out a strategy. Mrs Mooney got all excited whenever Blue managed to win a trick.

'I tell you, Blue, you're picking it up. I'll soon have you playing poker and winning.'

Blue grinned. She liked Jimmy's mother and the card-playing. While they played they talked. Blue told her about running away to Galway and how Mary and Tommy were reunited, and about the Hickeys and the Maguires, and about losing Jess and about kind Sister Monica and the other girls in Larch Hill, and what had happened with Sister Regina the time she left the newspaper clipping on the floor in her office.

Mrs Mooney reminisced about her late husband Paddy, who was the best husband a woman could have, and her daughter Terry, who lived in Dundalk with her husband John and had four children, and confided how hard it was for Jimmy since his wife had run off to Manchester with an old boyfriend and had taken their little boy Danny with her.

Poor Jimmy, thought Blue. She imagined his little boy in England never getting to see his daddy.

* * *

'Don't tell me you have the child playing cards already?' joked Jimmy when he arrived home. Blue's stomach sank at the thought of what he'd say about her and what they would decide to do.

'Sit down, the dinner'll be ready in a minute,' said Mrs Mooney as she set out three place mats, and knives and forks, and Jimmy buried himself in the sports results in the evening newspaper.

The shepherd's pie was delicious, full of meat and gravy and creamy potato on top. Blue ate it as slowly as she could, to savour every minute of sitting around the table with them while Jimmy told them about the tourist who left one of his bags in the car and gave him an extra big tip for returning it to his hotel and Mrs Mooney praised Blue's card-playing abilities.

'Still raining outside?' asked Mrs Mooney.

'Hasn't let up all day.'

''Tis an awful night to be going back out in the rain and dark with the child. Maybe it would be best to let her sleep in the small room, just for the night, what d'ye think?'

Blue held her breath, waiting for his answer.

Jimmy Mooney hesitated, torn between doing what his heart told him and getting into trouble with the law.

'All right, Ma, she can stay the night but I'll have to take her back first thing in the morning after breakfast. We'll be in terrible trouble if I don't.'

Blue jumped up and threw her arms around his neck, kissing him on his big red cheek.

Mrs Mooney came up to check on her after she had settled in the comfy bed. The kind old woman brought her a glass of warm milk and a digestive biscuit. Blue lay, snuggled up under a layer of heavy woollen blankets and a feather quilt with three squashy pillows behind her head. She wore an old floral-patterned nightdress Mrs Mooney had given her and she had a warm hot-water bottle to cuddle up to as she gazed at the rosebud-patterned wallpaper and the gaily striped curtains, with the rain lashing down outside. She could hear from downstairs the sing-song voices of mother and son talking late into the night. She concentrated on every moment of warmth and comfort, so she could call it up in her imagination in the future. This was one time when there was no need to imagine herself in another place. Instead, she pretended that this was *her* room and this was *her* home.

Jimmy Mooney was quiet the next morning and Blue couldn't help but be nervous as she ate the creamy porridge and slice of brown bread for breakfast. Her own clothes and shoes were dry again.

'You'll come back soon to visit us, love,' said Nance Mooney kindly.

Blue nodded, not trusting herself to speak. She noticed that Jimmy had put on a clean shirt and tie and combed hair oil through his few strands of dark hair. Eventually he led her out to the narrow street of identical red-brick, terraced homes where his shiny black taxi cab was parked.

'You take care, love, and don't mind what any of those old rips of nuns say to you,' advised Nance Mooney. Blue flung herself into the broad arms, not wanting to leave.

'Come on, we've got to go,' urged Jimmy, and Blue sat into the front seat of the car beside him.

Blue was determined not to cry or beg or let herself down as she resigned herself to returning to the place where she had been raised.

There would be no more running away. No more escapes. Larch Hill was the only home she had and it was high time she accepted it. The nuns would kill her. They would make an example of her in front of the other girls and Sister Regina would have a suitable punishment planned for her. She tried not to shake when she thought about it, not wanting the fear to engulf her. Instead she thought about Mary and Tommy and prayed that both of them were okay.

Jimmy coughed. 'You understand, Blue, that Mammy and I wouldn't be suitable candidates to raise a child or foster one. Mammy's too old and I'm on my own since Sheila left me.'

'It's all right,' she sighed. 'I understand.'

'I already have a child, a little boy, Danny. He's almost six and I never get to see him.'

'Thank you and Mrs Mooney for taking me in and looking after me.'

'Will you be all right?'

She watched the buses and cars in front of them.

'I'll be fine,' she lied. 'Fine.'

The gates looked bigger, the wall even higher, as the car pulled up the driveway of Larch Hill. Mr Mooney came to a halt outside the front door. Blue swallowed hard as dread clenched her muscles. Jimmy, looking uncomfortable, opened the car door and walked with her up the steps to ring the bell. They heard distant footsteps on the tiled floor. Sister Agnes opened the door, her eyes widening when she saw Blue.

'I found the child wandering along by the quays,' offered Jimmy Mooney. 'She was in a right state. Shock, I reckon.'

'Thank you very much, sir, for returning Bernadette to us. We've been frantic with worry about her and had alerted the relevant authorities,' said the nun. She smiled a false smile, her pale face taut with suppressed anger. 'You can leave the child with me. I will bring her straight to our mother superior to tell her the good news that the child has been found safe and well. We are very grateful for your good deed. I will look after her now as you have already given up more than enough of your time to bring her here.'

'What will happen her?' he asked gruffly.

'Happen?' The nun looked perplexed. 'Naturally, the child must learn that she cannot behave in such a fashion. Such things cannot be tolerated in a place like this. We have all the other children in our care to think of. She needs discipline and Sister Regina, our mother superior, will know what to do.'

Sister Agnes was trying to politely move the taxi driver out of the hall towards the door and back out to his car.

'If you'll excuse me, Sister,' his face had flushed red, the veins on his neck standing out above his shirt collar, 'I would like to meet Sister Regina. I think it's important that I talk to her myself.'

'She is very busy at present,' muttered the nun.

'Then I'll wait.' He stepped past Sister Agnes and lowered himself into a high-backed mahogany chair. 'I'm not leaving here till I speak to her.'

Sister Agnes was unable to disguise her annoyance.

'That child doesn't need punishing,' he explained slowly. 'I reckon she's had punishment enough.'

'Well, that is for us, her guardians, to decide,' replied the nun coldly.

'I wouldn't like to hear that one hair on the girl's head had been harmed, or that a finger had been laid on her,' the man said obstinately.

Sister Agnes moved her lips and face, but no words came out.

'Bernadette, go upstairs immediately and wait in your room,' she said eventually. 'I will tend to you in time, so stay there, do you hear?'

'Yes, Sister.' Blue threw a grateful glance at Jimmy Mooney, who, despite his discomfort, looked like he was prepared to sit for hours if he had to.

'You take care of yourself, Blue,' he called as she began to walk up the stairs.

CHAPTER 26

The Cell

She waited and waited in the empty dormitory but there was no sign of Sister Agnes or Sister Regina. She wondered what could be going on and what kind of awful punishment she could expect. The lunch bell went and from below came the heavy trooping of footsteps as the others come back from school for their midday meal.

Lil surprised her by coming upstairs to get her cardigan.

'Blue!' she shrieked. 'You're back! We thought we'd never see you again.'

Immediately the two girls fell into each other's arms.

'Where's Mary? Isn't she with you?'

'No. We went to Galway and we found Tommy. She wanted to stay and take care of him. We were upstairs in the dormitory in Saint Gerard's when we heard one of the brothers coming and I made a run for it. I escaped but Mary wouldn't leave him. I don't know what's happened her. Did you hear anything?'

'Not a word.'

'God, I hope she's okay.'

'But why did you come back?'

Blue sat on the corner of the bed, going over and over it in her head.

'I had no money and nowhere else to go,' she said bitterly.

'I'm glad you're back,' grinned Lil, her brown eyes sparkling. 'I missed you.' She could only stay a few minutes and then had to return downstairs. 'Wait till I tell everyone you're back, they won't believe it.'

Blue sat hunched and miserable on the mattress. So much for her great escape plans. Dreaming, that's all it was. She would never leave here, never. Not until she was sixteen. It was too long to wait.

Finally, Sister Regina came up to see her. She recognised the heavy step in the corridor and she prepared herself to become the focus for all the nun's rage and anger.

'So you came back!' the woman sneered. 'Decided that Larch Hill was your home – the only place that would take you in, probably.'

'Yes, Sister.'

'Don't you "Yes, Sister" me like that. I know what you're like. A troublemaker, a hothead! You incite others to get into trouble too. You encouraged Mary Doyle to go with you. Well, no doubt you'll be glad to hear that she was caught and that she and her brother have been moved to a children's home in Donegal.'

'Both of them have been moved?'

'Yes, that's what I said. I told Brother Benildus to lock the two of them up and throw away the key. I'll be sending a report about those Doyle children to whoever is in charge of them now. I'll mark their card.'

Blue was so relieved that Mary and Tommy had been kept together that she almost cheered. She might never see her friend again but at least Mary was with her brother. It was all she had ever wanted.

'Once again you have caused this order endless trouble and embarrassment. We had the Guards out looking for you and I had to inform the authorities and the head of the order of your disappearance.'

'I'm sorry, Sister.'

'Sorry! I take a dim view of your behaviour. You have let Larch Hill down and are a bad influence on the rest of the children here. If I had my way you would be moved to another children's facility, where they wouldn't suffer any of your nonsense. We have almost two hundred children here to look after and we don't have the time for troublemakers like you.'

'I'm sorry, Sister,' she whispered.

'Sorry! You don't even know the meaning of the word. You are to be at my office in two hours' time. I will deal with you then.'

The nun swished out of the room, the skirt of her long black habit flying as she turned away. Blue felt sick to the stomach, knowing that she would be punished severely.

Two hours later she stood outside the nun's office, trying to get her courage up to knock on the door.

'Enter!' Sister Regina called, when she finally managed it.

Blue tried to control the shaking that overwhelmed her as she stood in front of the nun's desk.

'Not as brave and cheeky as you were a few days ago, I see,' commented Sister Regina, who sat at her desk with her pen and papers spread out in front of her.

Blue, unsure what to say or do, said nothing. She was waiting for the order: 'hold out your hands'. Her fingers and hands were quivering and shaking and no matter how hard she tried she couldn't control them.

'Keep still!' insisted the nun.

Blue was determined not to cry or beg or break down. She wasn't going to give the nun the satisfaction of that. She looked down at the blue and red braided mat on the floor, trying to get her breath as Sister Regina stood up.

This time there was no leather, no strap, but the nun launched into a torrent of words telling her how valueless she was, that she was a nothing, that she would be out on the streets if it weren't for the charity of the order, calling her mother words Blue didn't even understand, only sensing the shame of their meaning. Like waves the words washed over her, almost knocking her down, and she thought of Jess smiling and waving to her to join her, to swim in the sea, saying her friend's name over and over in her head to block out the bad words as the nun ranted on and on telling her that no one wanted her or loved her and that she should be separated from decent children.

Blue could have kicked or spat at her or pulled the veil from the woman's head and scratched at her face and eyes, but instead she stayed still, listening to the frantic beat of her heart and the sound of her breath, knowing, somehow, deep inside her that the woman before her had little or no connection with the God she was supposed to pray to. Eventually the stinging snake of words stopped.

'What have you to say for yourself?'

'I'm sorry,' she whispered.

Sister Regina let out an exasperated sigh as she sat back into her chair.

'Anything else?'

'I am a child of God, and God loves me,' said Blue softly, words Sister Monica had once said to her somehow coming into her head. For a split second she thought that Sister Regina would pull out the leather strap and begin to beat her.

'Get out of here!' the nun ordered.

* * *

'Blue! Blue! Are you all right?' The voice pulled her from the faraway place, as she struggled to wake up.

'You've been asleep for ages,' grinned Sarah. 'You missed tea, but we kept you some.'

'I'm not hungry ...' she started to say, not wanting to deprive them of their food.

But Lil pulled a slice of bread and jam, lightly wrapped in a hanky, from her pocket and handed it to Blue.

'Thanks,' she said, her voice shaking.

'What did that bloody tormentor do to you?'

Blue didn't want to talk about it, there was no point. She looked around at the sea of faces clustered near her bed. Sarah and Lil and Big Ellen, even Annie and Carmel and Roisin – they were her friends, the only people in the world that cared about her. Tears began to run down her face again.

'I don't know why I'm crying,' she blubbered, feeling like a big eejit as Lil wrapped her arms around her.

'You're going to be all right, Blue, honest.'

'What's going on here?'

They all nearly jumped out of their skins when they looked up and saw the black habit and veil, relief washing over them when they realised it was Sister Monica.

'Bernadette O'Malley is back, Sister,' announced Annie.

'Well, isn't that good news, girls. The missing sheep has returned to the flock.'

She waited for the nun to give out to her, but there was no display of anger or temper. 'You girls had all better start getting ready for bed,' she warned instead. 'I believe Sister Agnes is on her way up.'

Everyone scattered to change into their nightclothes and wash their faces and hands and brush their teeth.

Blue sat wearily on the edge of her bed as Sister Agnes appeared. 'Bernadette O'Malley, what are you doing in this dormitory?'

'I sleep here, Sister,' she replied, confused.

'Not any more, you don't. You heard Sister Regina, she has made other arrangements for you. You are no longer allowed to share this room with the other girls.'

Blue stood up, embarrassed. 'But, Sister, where am I to sleep, then?'

'You are to follow me.'

The rest of the girls kept their eyes down as Blue left the large dormitory where she had slept for almost ten years.

'It is decided that you will sleep on your own, where you have no chance to influence the other girls with your bad behaviour.'

She followed Sister Agnes up the narrow back stairs, stopping outside a heavy wooden door. 'This is your room,' said the nun, pushing open the door.

The room was tiny, with just enough space for a narrow bed and a chair. A naked light bulb hung from the ceiling. The window was way above her head, too high for her to see out of. A multicoloured rag rug covered part of the floor, the only colour in the room. A chamber pot nestled under the iron bed frame.

'That is in case you are taken short during the night.'

'I don't understand.'

'Your door will be locked. It will be opened again by one of the sisters when we rise for early-morning mass.'

Blue could feel her heart plummet. She was going to be kept prisoner in this cell.

'It is for your own good,' offered the nun. 'We can't have you running away again.'

Sister Monica suddenly appeared on the stairway behind them, her eyes concerned as she looked at the room.

'There must be some mistake, Agnes,' she objected. 'This place isn't suitable for a child. It's meant for adult contemplation, prayer.'

'Sister Regina feels it is. If you have a problem about this, Sister, I suggest you take it up with her in the morning.'

'I shall do that,' said Sister Monica, looking flushed and annoyed.

Blue sat down on the bed.

'I'll sit with the child for a while,' offered the kind old nun. 'We'll pray together before she sleeps.'

Satisfied, Sister Agnes left.

'I'll try and sort things out in the morning, Bernadette,' she promised, but both of them knew that the head nun was not one to change her mind or back down on anything.

Over the next half hour Blue found herself telling Sister Monica about running away to Galway, about Mary and Tommy finding each other, and about Mr and Mrs Mooney and the small house on Iveagh Terrace.

'I ran away too, when I was twelve,' confided Sister Monica. 'I wanted to join Duffy's Travelling Circus.'

'The circus?'

'I wanted to be a bare-back rider or a trapeze artist. Could you imagine me swinging from a rope in the middle of the big top?' she chuckled.

Blue could.

'Luckily, my older sister discovered my plan and managed to haul me home before I got into too much trouble. The thing is, sometimes we all feel the need to run away.'

Blue felt strangely comforted for she liked and respected the thin, wiry little nun with her strange ways and habits.

'Bernadette, try not to fret alone in this room. The other girls and myself and the rest of the sisters are all still close by.'

She nodded, as Sister Monica bent down and kissed the top of her head. 'Sleep well, child.'

Blue lay totally still on the narrow bed. The room was so quiet. Her eyes were drawn to the patch of moonlight reflected through the high window. It was like being in a box, a caged animal. She felt as if her heart was broken, cracked right through by a jagged line. She stared at the wall, as the reflected shadows of clouds and stars and moonlight mingled and danced. She wished she still had the yellow book, especially tonight when she needed it so badly. She closed her eyes … the hut was small, the sound of wind and insects rustled in the grass roof above her, outside the animals moved in the dirt and dust making their way in the darkness to the water hole as the babies and children slept, but Teza sang with them, her body still warm from the sun as she clapped her hands and danced ...

CHAPTER 27

The Picnic

B ack at school the map on the board they used for geography reminded Blue of the great escape and the places she and Mary had travelled through: Kinnegad, Kilbeggan, Athlone ... Next year she would learn more geography when she went to the secondary school up the road.

Months passed. July was roasting hot and when August came Lil and Sarah and the rest of Blue's friends went away for the usual week's holiday to the summer home in Wexford while she had to stay behind to help in the nursery. Blue tried to pretend that it didn't matter when they told her about the fun they had had on the beach and Lil finally trying to learn to swim, tried to pretend she didn't give a toss about things like that because she was used to being alone. At night when she climbed into bed in her tiny, cramped room, she dreamed of faraway places – Africa, Asia, India, Alaska – and the lonesome world around her dissolved away.

It was a warm September Sunday when Sister Monica called her and told her to go to the front parlour.

'You have a visitor, Bernadette. Tidy your hair and put on a clean blouse, that's a good girl.'

She wondered who it could be and almost jumped with joy when she saw Jimmy Mooney, looking more uncomfortable than ever, sitting on a spindly armchair that looked set to break under his weight.

'How are you, girl? I hope the nuns are treating you right.'

She couldn't speak, didn't know what to say.

'I was wondering would you fancy coming out with me and Ma for the afternoon? That is, if you want to.'

Want to! She couldn't imagine anything better, but maybe the nuns wouldn't let her.

'I've already asked permission from Sister Monica,' he said, as if reading her mind.

'I'd better get my coat and change my shoes.' She was almost frightened to go lest he disappear and be gone when she got back.

'Don't worry,' he said, reading her mind again. 'I'll wait here for you, lass.'

Nance Mooney was sitting in the front seat of the black taxi and greeted her with a big hug.

'We were thinking of going to Dollymount strand for a bit of a walk and a picnic and we thought you might like to come with us.'

'Yes, please!'

'Jimmy doesn't get much time off at the weekends but I told him he needed to get out and get a bit of fresh air. Do us all good.'

Blue sat into the back of the car as Mrs Mooney talked nineteen to the dozen about her big win at Bingo the previous Tuesday.

'All my numbers came up, all of them. I had a full house in about six minutes.'

Blue didn't exactly know what the importance of the numbers or a full house was, but she congratulated the woman warmly.

As they drove out towards Dublin Bay, Jimmy pointed out various places to Blue. 'There's the Poolbeg lighthouse, Ringsend gas works. That island over there is called Ireland's Eye.'

She guessed he must know every street and road and building in Dublin.

Blue loved the way the sea shimmered in the sunlight and the waves rolled in and out, in and out, unchanging. She almost cheered when Jimmy turned off the roadway and drove across a road of sand and clay, the car finally pulling up on the grass above the beach.

They tumbled out of the car, and Mrs Mooney tied a red scarf around her head to protect her perm. Jimmy carried a rug and a wicker basket, while Blue took out the three cushions that were in the boot.

'Take off your shoes and socks,' warned Mrs Mooney before they set off to find their spot on the beach, 'or they'll be covered in sand.'

Blue followed her advice and rolled her white ankle-socks into the toe of her shoes, which she carried under her arm. The sand felt warm and she scrunched her toes in it.

''Tis good for your feet, gets rid of the rough skin and corns,' said Mrs Mooney.

'I'm sure Blue doesn't have corns, Ma,' Jimmy remarked.

They walked for a few minutes along the almost-empty beach, until Mrs Mooney finally decided on the perfect place to stop.

'Here will do nicely, Jimmy,' she said.

He spread out the tartan rug and flopped down beside her. Blue felt suddenly shy and awkward.

'Sit yourself down, pet,' urged Mrs Mooney, patting the cushion on the rug beside her.

Blue thought the beach was beautiful and was content to just sit and stare and soak it all in. In the distance the huge ferry-boat sailed across the Irish Sea towards England. She watched the seagulls toss and swirl in the sky above them, and the rippling white yacht sails flutter in the wind as they bobbed in Dublin Bay.

'Take big breaths of that sea air,' suggested Jimmy. 'Good for the mind and body.'

Blue stretched out in the warm sunshine.

'How about a paddle?' asked Mrs Mooney, after a while. 'I'm too old for swimming but I do enjoy a paddle. What about you?'

Blue didn't have to be asked twice and jumped up immediately. Nance Mooney rolled up the skirt of her dress and tucked it in the elastic of her white cotton knickers. She looked a sight but didn't seem to care. Blue rolled up the waistband of her own skirt, and together they put their toes into the freezing water. Blue almost jumped with shock as the icy water covered her feet and ankles.

'Ow! Ow! Ow!' they shouted in unison, laughing and screaming like two children as they ran in and out of the waves.

Jimmy appeared a few minutes later in a pair of large black swimming trunks and without hesitation ran straight into the water and dived under, ignoring their warnings about the cold. His big shoulders and dark head bobbed about in the water.

'He always loved swimming,' Mrs Mooney said approvingly. 'Used to swim in the Iveagh baths when he was your age.'

They waded out as far as they could towards where Jimmy was swimming. Envious, Blue watched Jimmy dive and splash like an otter. She kept a close eye on his dark head in the waves. Eventually he got out, his teeth chattering as he wrapped himself in a big green towel.

'Let's go for a run up along the beach to dry off,' he suggested.

Mrs Mooney backed out, but Blue and Jimmy raced along the seashore, the warm sun drying the salt water to a fine layer of white on their skin.

'I wish I could swim properly,' Blue said.

'I'll teach you,' he offered.

'Teach me?'

'Yes, next summer.'

She said nothing.

'I mean it. I'll bring you down here and we'll get you a costume, and, you'll see, in no time you'll be like those kids out there.' He pointed to some boys having swimming races a few yards out from the shore.

Blue blinked. He was talking about *next* summer, nearly a whole year away, as if she was going to be a part of his plans, his life. She said nothing as they stopped running and walked slowly back the way they had come, their footprints still imprinted on the sand.

Mrs Mooney had brushed all the sand off the rug and spread out the cushions again and opened the wicker picnic basket.

'I'm famished,' she declared. 'Sea air always gives me an appetite.'

Blue flung herself down on the rug and bit into a thick ham sandwich made with soft crusty bread and golden butter and a bit of lettuce.

'Want any mustard?'

She shook her head. It was perfect as it was. There were hard-boiled eggs still in their shells, which they peeled and ate dipped in salt, and juicy red tomatoes and Mrs Mooney's home-made buns. Then Jimmy took out the big flask and some plastic cups and poured them all some tea.

'Have you had enough to eat?' he asked eventually.

Blue had never had such a feast. 'I love picnics,' she shouted, her voice catching in the air.

When they had finished eating she helped Mrs Mooney to repack the battered wicker basket and wrap up the rubbish and brush the sand away. Jimmy stretched out on the rug, his hands under his head as he settled down to snooze in the sun.

Blue walked down near the water to feed some left-over crusts to a curious seagull who'd been hovering around. She bent down, picking up bits and pieces of old shells, a black stone and a round speckled grey one, all smooth and shiny from the sea; she found a lovely piece of driftwood too. She gathered them and put them in her pocket, souvenirs of the day out.

Before going home they all went for a final paddle, the tide almost out, and Blue wishing the day would never end.

'It was magic,' she sighed as she sat on the rug drying her feet with the stripey towel.

'You'll be back again,' reassured Mrs Mooney, shaking out her cardigan.

Blue blinked, not quite believing it.

'I meant it about teaching you to swim next summer,' declared Jimmy, standing barefoot on the sand, his skin burned pink with the sun, 'and about coming back to Dollymount and doing lots of other things besides.'

'Go on, tell the child,' urged Mrs Mooney.

'I talked to the nuns.' Jimmy Mooney was standing in front of Blue, his big face unusually serious. 'That Sister Regina and the other nun with the pointy face. We asked and we tried, we did everything we could, but they still said Ma and I can't foster you.'

Blue looked at the waves.

'We can't foster you because of my marital status and ...' he looked at his mother.

'Me being an old one,' said Mrs Mooney.

Blue could hardly breathe. What were they saying? What were they trying to tell her?

'But we *can* take you out. Take you home to Iveagh Street, have you visit at weekends and in the holidays ...' he trailed off '... that's if you like, of course. If you want to.'

If you like ...

'I suppose we could be a sort of a family, if you want to call it that,' he added huskily.

Blue jumped up from the sand and flung herself into his arms. Jimmy caught her and swung her high in a circle, going round and round, the sea and sand spinning madly.

Mrs Mooney was half-crying with happiness. 'Jimmy, I told you the child needed to be part of a family. Knew it the minute I laid eyes on her. She'll come and visit as often as she can, stay with us whenever she wants.'

'We know we're not the perfect family,' Jimmy said slowly. 'Not what you expected or deserve. We're just simple, ordinary people, but we do care about you and when the time comes and you are old enough to leave Larch Hill, you will have a place in Iveagh Street.'

Blue was overwhelmed with emotion. It was true: this wasn't what she had expected or imagined at all. A big man with red cheeks, and hairs that grew on his chest and arms, and had sunburned skin and smoked tobacco and had a mind like a map, and a fat old woman with permed grey hair who like to paddle with her skirt stuffed into her knickers and play cards. It wasn't what she had imagined at all, but somewhere deep in her hungry heart she knew that Jimmy and Nance Mooney were the exact people she wanted to have as family.

'Thank you,' she said hugging them both. 'Thank you … thank you …'

They sang all the way home and Jimmy bought three whipped ice cream cones to celebrate. Bursting with happiness, Blue savoured the sweet, creamy taste.

'I'll collect you next Sunday and maybe we might go for a walk in Stephen's Green. There's ducks there and swings and a slide.'

'And I'll cook something special, and make some more of my buns,' smiled Nance Mooney, trying to wipe her smeared hands clean with a hanky.

Blue leaned back against the leather car seat. She couldn't wait to get back and tell Lil and Sarah and Sister Monica the good news. At long last she had found ... well sort of found ... a family of her own.